Henry Bradford was born in Gravesend, Kent, in October 1930. His father had been a regular soldier in the Queen's Own Royal West Kent Regiment during the First World War, serving in the trenches in France and Belgium, until he was wounded in the battle of the Somme on the first of July 1916.

Mr Bradford met Henry's mother, Jessica Reynolds, in Colchester, Essex. They were married in the village church of Pebmarsh, Essex, and settled in Mr Bradford's home town of Gravesend, where they had nine children, Henry being the eighth child.

As a child Henry had a sparse, primitive education, as did most children of that era, because of poor teaching methods, and also because he was evacuated twice during the Second World War, once to Dereham, Norfolk, on the third of September 1939, then to Totnes, Devonshire, on the fourteenth of June 1940.

In Devonshire, Henry was injured in a farm accident that turned to septicaemia and necessitated his having to spend a year in Torbay and Exeter orthopaedic hospitals, before his being discharged in July 1941, when he returned home to Gravesend with what became a lifelong permanent disability.

On his leaving school in September 1944, at the age of fourteen years, Henry was employed in numerous jobs before following his grandfather, father and brothers into the port transport industry in March 1954 as a Registered Dock Worker with the London Dock Labour Board. Then, after having been seriously injured in a shipboard accident in April 1960, Henry attended night classes for two years (at the behest of the LDLB welfare officer, Mr D. J. Foley J. P.), before applying and being accepted as a post-graduate diploma student at the London School of Economics and Political Science.

After graduation, Henry returned to the docks where, during 1964-65, he wrote a comprehensive labour employment plan for the permanent employment of all registered dock workers.

Henry married in December 1955, Iris Kathleen Mann. They had two children, Dawn and Roland. Henry retired from the port transport industry in December 1968 due to the numerous injuries he had sustained in dock working accidents, and his war time evacuation injury; he had spent thirty-two years employed in the port transport industry, working in every conceivable job both on the docks and in clerical work as an Overseas Ships Tally clerk with dock stevedore companies, and as a ships clerk with the Port of London Authority.

After his enforced retirement, Henry was advised by a literary friend that he should write stories about his experiences and vast knowledge of London's docklands and, except for a story, "Animal Crackers in Country Parkland" about corruption in national and local government, his memories appear in print only in his series of books "Tales of London's Docklands", that can best be described as historical tales of dock work and dock workers in the mid-20th Century.

Henry T. Bradford

MEN OF THE RIVER

Tales of London's Docklands

AUSTIN MACAULEY PUBLISHERS™

LONDON • CAMBRIDGE • NEW YORK • SHARJAH

A CIP catalogue record for this title is available from the British Library.

ISBN 9781787104914 (Paperback)
ISBN 9781787104921 (E-Book)
www.austinmacauley.com

First Published (2017)
Austin Macauley Publishers Ltd.
25 Canada Square
Canary Wharf
London
E14 5LQ

Author's Note

I have to *come clean* with you, the reader of these tales, and state categorically that during my many years working in the Docklands of the Port of London as a docker, crane driver/winch driver, assistant ship worker, Overseas Ship Tally clerk, (OST), and ship's clerk. Every day was a learning curve, a lesson, a lesson that could never have been learnt or experienced in any other working environment, at least not within an industrial work setting. The simple reason for this was because of the nature in the variances of the different types of work, and the variety of skills, tools, and equipment required to carry out such diverse work operations.

So, before I go on to explain some of the work and background setting of the Docklands, I must also explain my other pre-occupations when on study leave from the docks. That is my time spent at the London School of Economics and Political Science reading for a Diploma in Personnel Management (now, so I understand, a discipline re-named Human Resources); at the West Kent College reading for a Certificate of Qualification in Social Work; at London's South West College reading for a Certificate in Method Study; Thurrock Technical College for a Certificate in The Principles of Port Operations; the University of Kent at Canterbury reading for a Diploma in Social Work and Physical Handicap, and of my eighteen plus years serving as a magistrate in Kent. All of these academic exercises were undertaken while I was still a Registered Port Worker, under the agency employment jurisdiction of the London Dock Labour Board within the Port of London.

Now it will be obvious to the reader the reason for this curious situation was the uniqueness of the socio-industrial work places, which were the enclosed Docklands, with their warehouses and transit sheds, with all the facilities required for loading ships with export cargoes. Or, discharging ships laden down with imported freight; the riverside wharves that serviced short sea trading vessels, lighters and barges; deep water jetties which in some circumstances were themselves used for housing cargoes, and the various sorts of working conditions that prevailed within those work places. Dock workers, as were all other workers employed in the docks, were constantly under the scrutiny of uniformed port authority police officers, plain clothed detectives, police informants, customs officers and customs watches and their informants, and no doubt other unseen eyes and ears that were never detected, at least by my informants.

On the other hand, different docks within the docklands handled different cargoes that were either shipped out of, or imported into, those docks from many overseas countries. Such import and export operations were the sole province of the many individual shipping companies, or conference line ships, that handled those merchants' goods who traded them. The personnel too, that made up the work forces within those dock workplaces, became specifically expert in the commodities they handled.

As, for example, in the Port of London's Surrey Commercial Docks, it was "deal porters" who discharged timber, mainly from short sea traders, with the timber coming mainly from Sweden and Russia. The Royal Victoria Docks was the main meat importing facility for ships trading with South America. The Royal Albert Docks for meat imports from, and exports to South Africa, Australia and New Zealand. The West India and Millwall Docks serviced ships sailing to, and returning from, the Mediterranean and Middle Eastern countries. Short sea traders sailed between Denmark and the riverside wharves by Tower Bridge on London's north bank; and Tooley Street wharves and cold storage warehouses on the south bank of the Thames. They were vessels that brought with them loins of pork, bacon, butter and other meat and dairy products.

On the other hand, some twenty miles downriver from the major docks of the Port of London, Tilbury Docks was noted for its imports of tea, wet and dry skins, crushed bones, bales of sisal, jute, hemp and gunnies. Imports were brought from India and Sri Lanka (formally known as Ceylon). Tilbury Docks was also the home port for passenger liners that traded with Australia up until the nineteen sixties, when the P&O and Orient shipping lines merged and transferred to the port of Southampton.

The West African Conference Line, whose ships traded with most ports down the west coast of Africa, moved down river from the pool of London to Tilbury Docks in nineteen fifty-seven. Its ships, always fully laden, sailed outward bound with general cargoes of wire crates filled with crockery, cases and cartons of manufactured goods of all descriptions, thousands of tons of bags of cement, cars, lorries, tractors and machinery of all kinds. When they returned, it was with freights of logs, cut timber, ground nuts, palm kernels, chests of tea, sacks of cocoa and coffee beans, yams, bananas, and various other commodities.

In order of seniority in the control of the dock workers, it was ship workers who were in charge of all registered dockworkers that manned ships. That is, crane or winch drivers who operated the mechanical equipment; top-hands who controlled the actions of crane and winch drivers (dockers were members of the Transport & General Workers Union, the white union); stevedores (members of the Stevedores & Dockers, blue union) who did the real work, and gearers who looked after the stevedore company's equipment. Quay foremen were in charge of the quayside receiving and/or freight delivery gangs.

Most of the men employed in the docks were drawn from dock working families, families that lived close to the docks in "back-to-back hovels" or blocks of tenement flats situated within walking distance of the dock gates.

To be more specific about those docks and wharves work places, they were ships holds, freight carrying lighters or sailing barges holds; enclosed dock quayside, warehouses or transit sheds; rail wagons or lorry platforms; riverside jetties or wharfs. For those men who worked on the river as tugboat-men, lighter-men, sailing barge masters and mates, or in the docks or afloat on the river as dockers or stevedores, they were such a diverse body of worldwide experienced travellers: merchant seamen and military war veterans who could not be found in such numbers in any other industry. They were men who between them had been, seen, and done almost anything and everything it was possible for ordinary men to do. Between them, what they did not know about life's miseries and blessings wasn't really worth knowing, because they were all survivors of the greatest of human tragedies, unrelenting worldwide warfare. In fact they were extraordinary men from ordinary backgrounds—those men of the river Thames and the London Docklands; and I hasten to say all the other docklands and ports throughout the British Isles.

What is more, because of the recruitment system used in the employment of Registered Dock Workers, as under the "Dock Workers (Regulation of Employment) Acts", regulations were carried out by the National Dock Labour Board (NDLB) through various Port Dock Labour Boards. A Government set up and controlled dock-workers' employment/unemployment agency, known more specifically by the registered work force as "The Dockers Dole House". There were always, as I have explained above, many diverse forms of dock work employment, carried out in different docks, situated in localities within the port, on different ships with their different varieties of cargoes. More often than not working with different men, in different localities, sometime on allocation to different docks, or wharves or jetties along the river banks, or in the tideway afloat, or even on occasions in a different port. And, too, often there was no work at all.

These slack periods, when work was scarce, caused despondency and hardship to dock workers' families. Misery that could only be measured by the poverty it caused to the women and children of the Men of the River and of the Docklands. To my mind, a politically unforgivable crime against the wealth producing people of this country.

Of course, this situation was due in the main to the over recruitment of personnel. It was in fact a lack of forward manpower planning that should have been based on shipping movements, not on rule of thumb stated labour requirements made by the port employers, who often stood by watching men jump on each other's backs, trying to get ship workers or quay foremen to "take hold of their attendance books".

It was a problem that could have been overcome by a centralised shipping movement system of manpower control, that should have been carried out under the jurisdiction of the various port authorities, as it was in Japan and South Africa. But that, it would appear, was too simple a solution to such a diverse labour employment problem.

So the NDLB was set up under the Dock Workers (Regulation of Employment) Act as an employment agency for the benefit of the shipping industry by government to register, and administer, dock worker dissipation in employment with a total disregard for the waste of manpower caused by a separate, bureaucratically administered employment agency. This was paid for directly by a levy of between 15% and 17.5% of dock workers gross earning to oversee dock working manpower employment at a time of Britain's greatest manpower shortages in most other industries, at the conclusions of hostilities after the Second World War.

Incidentally, many of those men that had come to work in the docklands had various other skills they had brought with them from their previous occupations before being "called up" for military service. They all had stories to tell of their military escapades in any of the many units that made up the British armed services, if one could get them to talk about them, that is. There were also included among the dockworkers men who had seen service throughout the war in the merchant navy. They, too, could tell tales of the hazards of sailing in convoys, of attacks on convoys by "wolf packs" of German U-boats, again if one could get them motivated to talk about them.

So I'm sure you, the reader, will understand just how difficult it was for an *interloper* such as myself not to fail to appreciate my own indoctrination into such a wealth of intelligence and experience that was to be gained from working with those men who had spent the whole of their lives being educated, as Jack Dash, the Port of London Dock Workers' Trade Union Liaison Chairman used to say, by their many and varied experiences in "The University of Life". If nothing else, one appreciated the stories they told, their sometime sadistic jokes and tricks they pulled on each other, their work skills, their bloody-minded sense of humour, and their physical stamina. All of which were kept hidden away from the general public behind high brick walls, or latticed wooden fences, that were the enclosed confines of the Docklands of the Port of London.

Contents

Ginger Fallbrook's Shiny Eight and We Dirty Half Dozen

Now to put you in the picture, Ginger Fallbrook was a ship worker employed by a renowned Port of London stevedore company, a company to be known (for the purpose of this tale) by the trade name of Muttons. However, it was a company better known by dockers and stevedores alike, who worked for that firm either as volunteers or pressed men (pressed men being those men allocated to that company by the sector's dock labour board manager), as Muttons for Buttons. A statement which simply means, of course, it was a stingy, penny-pinching company, whose ship workers and quay foremen were renowned for doing us piece working dockers and stevedores out of every last farthing they could sting (cheat) us out of.

Well to put you in the picture in relation to this story, it so happened that a loading ship had arrived in Tilbury docks berthed against a dummy, a floating pontoon that allowed Thames lighters and sailing barges to berth between it and the quay. The vessel was berthed almost opposite to Muttons' dock offices. Of course, we dockers were delighted the ship had been diverted to Tilbury docks away from its normal loading berth in London's Royal Albert docks. The reason for this being she was taking on board a large freight of cement cargo that was to be brought directly from the

Blue Circle cement factories on the opposite side of the river Thames at Northfleet, so there was a chance at least some of my newly demobilised, conscripted ex-servicemen workmates and I would get a job. Hopefully?

I have to say hopefully because we younger, newly recruited dockers, were known by the sobriquet of the "Dirty Half Dozen" by Muttons' ship workers and quay foremen. This being due in no small measure to our rebellious attitude to their authority, which means in fact we would not allow them to cheat us out of our piecework earning, or day work hours pay attributed to work stoppages. So, more often than not we were left in the Dock Labour Compound to kick our heels, while we waited to be allocated by the Dock Labour Board manager to some crap job within the Port of London; low paid jobs that none of the other Registered Dockers wanted. That is within docklands the great metropolis us new recruits had never heard of before becoming Registered Dock Workers.

However, on this day, for this particular ship, Ginger Fallbrook was on the call stand to "pick up" (employ) a full complement of ships gangs. That was three gangs of twelve men, and two gangs of thirteen men (two pro-rata winch drivers) to man five hatches, sixty-two men in all. Of course Ginger Fallbrook, as did all his contemporary ship workers and quay foremen colleagues, had what was known in those days as their "Shiny Eights". The "Shiny Eights" (men referred to in The Devlin Report on the port transport industry as Blue Eyed Boys), being his preferred "down holders", whom he picked up at the call stands in the Dock Labour Compound before taking on anyone else to man his ship. Unfortunately, it was not unusual for men in the scramble to get work to push, shove, jostle and even resort to fisticuffs, in their attempt to get a job.

On such occasions as this therefore, it was difficult for ship workers to get the Attendance Books of the men they wanted. So Ginger Fallbrook's "Shiny Eight" had worked out an identification system to overcome this problem. This was by the simple means of them all wearing white caps so that when Ginger came into the Dock Labour Compound, his "Shiny Eight" would muster en-block beside the "pick up point" and not move away from the muster railing until all their attendance books were in Ginger Fallbrook's hands. Only then would they give way to the other dockers, who would be pushing and shoving each other, so as to get near enough to the "call on stand" in the too-often-forlorn hope of getting "picked up" for a few days of what can best be described as virtual slave labour.

It was in this dog-eat-dog environment that we younger, unmarried men would let our brother dockers battle it out for a job. Then if must be, get ourselves allocated to work and take our chances as to what tainted job we were allocated to. On this day we were sent to Ginger Fallbrook's loading ship, whose main export cargo was to be Blue Circle Ball Dog cement, packaged in hundred weight brown paper sacks.

When we arrived at the ship's side, Ginger had already "told off" the other gangs to their respective hatches, placing his "Shiny Eight" down in Number two hold, which was the ship's main hatch—he visibly winced when he saw us scruffy, unkempt, long haired yobbos turn up as we sauntered our way along the quay towards his loading ship. The "Dirty Half Dozen" had arrived on the scene. His immediate reaction was: 'Holy Christ! Then. You lot can go to Number one hold. There's a lighter of cement under

19

plumb ready and waiting for you, the "barge hands" are already in the lighter making up sets of cement. Charlie Goodman is your down-hold foreman. He's up on the deck waiting for you.' Then before any of us had a chance to have a verbal harangue at him he nipped across the dock road into Muttons' offices, vanishing faster than a scared rabbit disappears into its warren.

Now I have to state that although we were referred to as the "Dirty Half Dozen" there were only five of us present at the time of this tale, so Charlie Goodman actually made up the sixth down holder. What's more, Charlie was without doubt one of the most experienced down hold foremen who worked in Tilbury docks. He was a quiet man who everyone respected, including us five of the "Dirty Half Dozen".

As we slouched our way along the deck towards Number one hatch, a smile broke out across Charlie's face, and he threw his hands up in the air as much as to say, "Christ! What have I done to deserve this?" Then he said: 'Right. Let's get the hatches and beams off, lads, we're going into the lower hold.'

It took us about half an hour to clear the deck, upper 'tween deck, and lower 'tween deck of their beams and hatch covers. No sooner had we clambered down into the lower hold than there was a set of cement hanging over our heads.

'We'll use these first sets to make a table,' said Charlie, 'We'll work side and side—port and starboard—from the wings out towards the square of the hatch. We've got a good team of barge hands and crane driver, let's set up a steady rhythm.' With that last order, he waved his hand to the top hand for the crane driver to lower the first set of cement, from which we made a table on which to land the following sets. Then we began the laborious task of walking the hundredweight bags of cement into the wings of the ship, starting against the fore-end bulkhead.

As the sets of cement came over, one after another, at regular intervals of one every two minutes, we scruffy yobbos of the "Dirty Half Dozen" laughed, joked, knocked each other as we passed from the loading bed to the stowage, while Charlie went about the job of levelling the stowage ready for the next consignment of cargo. This work and antics went on until "Beer Ho," when we all went ashore to get a mug of tea or coffee and a sandwich or bread roll from the Port Authority "Mobile Canteen Van".

As we approach the Mobile Canteen Van, Jean, the tea lady, looked down at us from her raised platform and laughed. 'What church building have you lot climbed down from,' she jested. 'You all look like stone statutes now you're plastered all over in cement dust,' but, she continued, 'I must say it's an improvement on your usual scruffy working clothes. Those old patched up service uniforms you're wearing look quite decent now they're covered in cement dust. The dust has covered up the holes in your clothes, and the patches too,' and she was laughing as she continued. 'Grey hair suits you lads. It gives you that soon-to-be extinguished look. That would please Muttons' ship workers no end, now wouldn't it?'

Jean was renowned for her wit and charm—she always joked and flirted with us dockers—but she was wide and wise to the work in the docklands; she knew where to draw a line under her wise cracking as she said:

'Come on lads, you must have parched throats swallowing all that cement dust—tea or coffee?'

'What's the difference Jean?' said Eric, my erstwhile workmate of long ago. 'The tea and coffee always taste like

21

a urine cocktail, and that's when we've not been working on cement. Just pour out whatever comes to hand, sweet heart.'

'For your information Eric, my darling,' she said. 'I thought that a man with even your limited education could work out the difference between the tea and coffee. Isn't it plainly obvious? The coffee's half a pence dearer than the tea,' then she laughed.

We drank our tea (or was it coffee—it was hard to tell the difference between them except for the price) and slowly returned back to the ship. As we made our way along the deck past Number two hatch, we chanced to look down into the 'tween deck. Ginger Fallbrook's Shiny Eight were still sitting on the wooden hatch covers drinking the tea their tea boy had made. (Regular ships gangs always had their tea on board ship, so as to save time and get back to work quickly). When they saw us looking down at them, some of them burst out laughing. One of them called up:

'How are you "Dirty Half Dozen" getting on? Have you got the hatches and beams off yet?'

We just gave them the V sign with our fingers without retorting, and returned to our cement-loading job in the lower hold where Charlie, our erstwhile down hold foreman, was waiting for us. Within seconds of getting back to work, there was a set of cement on its way, like the Sword of Damocles, it drifted inextricably down the open hatchway, on its inevitable way to join us. We soon got back into the rhythm of trudging bags of cement from the landing table, into the stowage area in the ship's wings. Well at least we did until about 11:00 a.m., when the electric crane decided to pack up by its motor over-heating and blew a fuse—or something. It was then that the "top-hand" (Hatchway Man) called down to us:

'You had better go to lunch. The Port of London Foreman has sent for an electrician, but he's tied up on another job. I'll see you back here at 1:00 p.m.' Then we heard the footfalls of his boots, as he marched off along the steel deck. It was then that we made our way up the three steel ladders of the lower hold, lower 'tween and upper 'tween decks, then through the booby hatch onto the ship's deck. We were just in time to see our "top-hand" scooting along the quay on the peddle of his bicycle, before he disappeared behind the rear end of a transit shed.

'Where shall we go for lunch?' said Eric. 'The Port Authority canteen doesn't open until 11:45 a.m.'

'Let's go to one of the cafés outside the docks,' Harry, another member of our "Dirty Half Dozen", suggested.

So, without another word we made our way out of the docks. We walked slowly past a Port of London Authority (PLA) police box, where a port authority police officer eyed us up and down as though we were convicted criminals, trying to escape from prison. But he chose not to call us into his cosy box, no doubt not wishing to get himself, or his temporary billet, plastered with that dirty grey dust we were smothered in.

We chose a café known as "Miss Winne's", bought a meal, and whiled away our time until near 1:00 p.m. when it was time to return to work. As we walked past the barge our barge hands were working from, we notice they had made up several sets of cement before they had left for lunch. So as soon as we had returned to the ship's hold—there was a set of that grey physical torment hanging over our heads— the Sword of Damocles had returned.

Once we had again got back into a steady rhythm, plodding our way from the landing bed to the stowage area, a distance that was getting shorter as we progressed inboard from the wings to the centre of the hatch, the rate of loading the cement got faster. By the time "Beer Ho" was called at about 2:30 p.m., we had worked our way into the square of the hatch. The lighter we had been working on was now empty, and the lighter-man was floating it out of its berth, making ready to float a loaded craft in. But now the rest of the afternoon and evening would be something like a teddy bear's picnic, compared to the morning's long trudge humping bags of cement out to the ship's wings.

As we climbed up the three steel ladders from the lower hold, out onto the ship's deck through the booby hatch, we were in high youthful spirits. Passing the Number two hatch we gave Ginger Fallbrook's "Shiny Eight" our V sign, before scampering down the ship's gangway to join the queue at the mobile tea van. Jean was busily pouring out cups of tea and coffee, and passing down lumps of bread pudding or cakes—and bread rolls with various fillings, that had no doubt been left over from her morning's foray, against the gastronomic attacks of hunger that hard work brings about to those of us who are forced by economic circumstances to dabble at it.

Jean's first words to us, as she laughed, were, 'Well they can't call you the "Dirty Half Dozen" now, can they? Look at you. Your mothers won't let you in the house when you go home tonight, you're absolutely plastered in cement.' Then she lowered her voice to a whisper and said, 'The rumour is Ginger Fallbrook's "Shiny Eight" aren't doing very well. If you beat them for tonnage, I think he'll throw himself in the dock. He'll never live it down if you "Dirty Half Dozen" are seen to do more tonnage than his "Shiny Eight".' Then she smiled, touched the side of her nose, then winked at us. It was obvious she was taunting us to beat Ginger Fallbrook's top gang, in the tonnage stakes that is. This caused Eric to stroke the side of his chin before saying:

'Yes! That would be a laugh. Let's give it a whirl. Come on let's get back to work.'

So, without another word we dashed off along the quay, scramble back up the ship's gangway onto the deck, ran past Number two hatch where Ginger Fallbrook was gaping down the hold, and remonstrating with one of the ship's gang. As we passed their open hatch we gave them the V sign with both hands, then scurried down through the Number one booby hatch on our way to the lower hold, where Charlie, our down hold foremen, was ready and waiting for us:

'Well, lads,' he said, 'all we've got to do now is fill in the square of the hatch. We'll work aft, away from the fore-end bulkhead. We should finish loading this section by the time we knock off.' It was then the first set of cement came down the hold, followed at regular intervals of two minute by others. But as I have already pointed out, it was a "picnic" compared with the morning slog, back and forth between the landing bed and the ship's outer wings of the lower hold.

At about 5:00 p.m., the top-hand shouted out there was to be a change of craft. The lighter-man was floating the dead (empty) craft out, and was about to bring a loaded lighter back under the cranes plumb. This gave us members of the "Dirty Half Dozen" just enough time, to nip up to the ship's galley, to scrounge a drink of water. As we passed Number two hatch, we took time to glance down at Ginger Fallbrook's "Shiny Eight". They were squatting round their battered teapot, slurping from mugs of tea. Like us, they were heavily coated with cement dust. A grey dust that clung to their clothes, and stuck to their heads and arms. Streaks of white skin showed on some parts of their faces, where sweat had run down in small rivulets, washing the cement dust away. It was as though they had each been dipped in a gluey grey batter, in some back street fish and chip shop—ready for being dropped in the fryer. A couple of them looked up at us through heavy, tired eyes, and gave us the V sign, but said nothing. We, on the other hand, went to the galley. The ship's cook was kind enough to give us a mug of water each, after which we quickly returned to our task at Number one hatch, lower hold, where a set of cement was already being lowered onto the landing bed at Charlie's instigation. The last phase of our day's work had begun.

Charlie, who hardly ever spoke, the exception being to give an order said:

'The craft that's just been berthed is carrying 80 tons of cement. We should be able to empty it before we knock off work tonight, if we put our backs to it.'

However, though the job was easier now we were working in the square of the hatch. The last eight hours slog was beginning to tell. There was no more larking about, no more laughter. The only sounds that could be heard in the lower hold, was the thumps as bags of cement were dropped into place under foot. It was about 6:30 p.m., the top-hand called down, 'There's only three sets left in the lighter, Charlie. I've rigged the "dolly-brook" up to a winch wire (a large tent that covered the hatch in case of rain). So as soon as you have finished these sets, come up on deck an' we'll cover up the hatch.'

We quickly finish stowing the three sets, wearily made our separate ways up the three steel ladders from the lower hold into the upper 'tween deck, then through the booby hatch onto the deck, where the top-hand was already raising the "dolly-brook" over the hatch. It didn't take us long to tie the "dolly-brook" in place, and make our way ashore. Ginger Fallbrook's "Shiny Eight" were in the process of covering up their hatch, making ready to go home; their OST clerk was still on the quay when I stepped off the ship's gangway.

'How have Fallbrook's old fogies performed today, Peter?' I asked their clerk.

'Three hundred and sixty tons,' he replied. Then he said, 'How did you "Dirty Half Dozen" get on?'

'I've no idea,' I replied, 'our clerk's already gone over to the office with his tally sheets. But I'll tell you when I get the "tick note" (a tick note was a record of the previous day's work record) in the morning.'

Post Script:
On the following day it was business as usual, more cement. There was to be a thousand tons stowed in Number one hold; six hundred tons in the lower hold, with four hundred tons in the two 'tween decks. During "Beer Ho" we went ashore to the mobile canteen, to get mugs of tea or coffee. Jean was again the tea lady, and she greeted us with:

'You're in for a surprise when you get your "tick note". I overheard Muttons' ship workers ribalding Ginger Fallbrook in their mess room when I took their food in to them earlier this morning. It was something to do with yesterday's tonnages. You'll find out when you get your "tick note". But I can tell you, Ginger Fallbrook was less than pleased. I heard him say something about levelling the score with day work hours, I don't know what he meant.'

Having heard that warning, we thanked Jean for her news, then made our way back to the ship. It was soon after

"Beer Ho", our mid-morning break, that Charlie, our revered down hold foreman, came down the hold with our previous day's "tick-note". He seemed to be overjoyed with the tonnage we had achieved, over four hundred tons, a record using cement nets instead of cement boards. He was especially pleased, for as he pointed out we were a "scratch gang", not a regular ships gang. Then he passed me the "tick-note".

After perusing the "tick note" for a few seconds, I passed it round my workmates of the "Dirty Half Dozen" before telling Charlie, 'I'm not having this. Where's that damn ship worker?'

'On deck at Number 1 hatch talking to the top-hand,' he replied.

I said no more but scrambled up the three steel ladders like a bullet from a rifle. As I tumbled out of the bobby hatch in my haste, I almost fell on top of Ginger Fallbrook in my progression. He was making his way along the ship's deck when I managed to confront him with, 'Now Ginger, what's this, there are no day work hours on this "tick note",' I told him, as I brandished the "tick note" under his nose (Day work hours were a contractual entitlement under piece-working agreements, if working time was interfered with for any genuine reason).

'Day work hours,' he blurted out, 'your gang loaded over four hundred tons of cement yesterday. It's not humanly possible for any gang to do that tonnage in a day.'

'You mean because your "Shiny Eight" only managed to load three hundred and sixty tons yesterday, that you were made to look a fool, because we maligned members of the "Dirty Half Dozen", beat them at their own game by loading over forty tons more than them? Come off it, Ginger,' I said, 'I want three hours' day work added to that "tick-note".'

It was then that he flew into one of his famous tantrum. (Oh! Did I forget to tell you about Ginger's tantrums? That was when he would throw his hat on the deck, then jump on it). Well. When the silly sot had finished doing a war dance on his hat, and had stepped back, puffing hot air from his *gills* due to his exertion, I casually kicked the hat into the air. The hat, a now flattened soft cap, (more commonly known among us members of the wealth-producing lower classes as a "cheese-cutter"), took off from the ship's deck like a miniature flying saucer. It floated majestically across the top of the dock water for several hundred yards, carried in its flight by a gentle sea breeze, before alighting on top of a crested wave. It then went floating slowly away along the dock, with the flotsam, jetsam and dirty oil-covered dock water. Ginger Fallbrook stood by the ship's deck rail watching in disbelief, mouth agape, as his hat slowly filled with water, and disappeared from sight.

'You stupid idiot,' he yelled at me, 'look what you've done to my hat.'

'Idiot or not,' I told him. 'I still want three hours' day work money on that "tick note".' But I may just as well have been talking to the sea breeze, because Ginger Fallbrook, in his melancholia state of mind, was just not listening to me.

A Musical Interlude (Dockers Style)

'Three spoonfuls of sugar?' Brains, the gang's tea boy, blurted out, 'You don't take sugar in your tea, Tom.'

'No I don't usually, do I? But that's when we're not working on any other job than a Tate and Lyle sugar loading boat,' replied Tom, the ship's gang's "down-hold foreman", angrily.

'So what's the difference in this job and any other job we do?' Brains asked, in all innocence. 'It's all damn hard labour. Well, Tom? Isn't it?'

'Yes. I make you right there, Brains. But haven't you ever worked on one of these sugar loading jobs with me before?' Tom asked him.

'No I haven't,' came the curt and suspicious reply. 'Why, what's wrong with it?'

'What's right with it more like? Two shillings and seven pence a ton, that's what's wrong with it. Or, to be more precise, three pence per man per ton (that's roughly one new penny per man in today's money value). And even though the sugar is in two-hundred weight hessian sacks, those damn old dilapidated Wellman cranes up there on the riverside jetty, can only manage to lift thirty hundredweight at a time, and they're so damn slow. We've only got five hundred tons of sugar to load into this hold, but it's going to take us at least two days to load it at the rate we're working. The tide's falling too, so the distance between the lighter on the inside of the jetty, and the ship berthed on the riverside, is getting greater by the minute; and unless we can rig up a "yo-yo" (two cranes acting as a union purchase feeding a larger one), the time between a set of sugar leaving the lighter, and arriving down here in the ship's hold, will be getting longer and longer. So, take my word for it, Brains. The only way we're going to earn any money on this rotten job is by heaping sugar in our tea, and that's what I'm doing. So stick another spoonful in before the tea gets too cold to dissolve it.'

'Oh, give up moaning, Tom,' one of the ship's gang said, 'we'll be out of this job in a couple of days; that's if the weather stays fine that is.'

'Yes,' replied Tom, 'and that's another thing isn't it, if the weather stays fine. But you don't think the ship worker came into the Dock Labour Compound to pick up a gang out of the goodness of his heart, do you? No bloody fear he didn't, them in the office have been listening to the weather forecast. You can bet your bottom dollar it's going to rain before the day's out, you wait and see if I'm not right.'

Tom's ships gang had been unfortunate enough to be in the National Dock Labour Board Compound (NDLB), on the free for all usual scramble for jobs, when a labour contractor's ship worker had dashed into the compound just seconds before the 1:00 p.m. "call on" had finished. In a rush to pick up a "double-banking gang" for a ship that was loading Tate and Lyle sugar (double banking simply means two ships gangs working down the same ships hold).

The vessel was berthed at Tilbury Deep Water Riverside Cargo Jetty, and Tom's "ships gang" had volunteered for the

31

job as a complete gang. Simply because had they chosen to lodge their "attendance books" in at the NDLB office when the tannoy system blared out "all books in", they knew from long and bitter experience it would mean they'd be split up as a "ship's working gang" and that it could be weeks, or even months, before they finally got back together as a working unit.

So there we were, squatting on warm sacks of granulated sugar that had recently been towed down river in steel lighters to Tilbury Docks Deep Water Riverside Jetty, direct from the Tate and Lyle sugar refinery in Silver town, North Woolwich. The sugar we were loading was coming from a lighter moored between the shore-side of the jetty, and the dock river wall, much of which we had already stowed in the wings of the "lower 'tween deck" by mid-afternoon. But now it was our tea break (more commonly known as "Beer Ho" time in those far off days in the nineteen-fifties). So, we were squatting on the sacks of warm Tate and Lyle sugar, close to the stringer boards near the ship's outer steel plates, moping like chastised school children over the loss of our piecework earning opportunity. It was then as we were comfortably installed in our warm squat, slowly sipping at mugs of hot *sweet* tea, provided by Brains, our gang's "tea-boy", with water scrounged from the ship's galley, tea filched from our last tea discharging job, tins of thick Libby's milk likewise obtained, and sugar liberated from a recently landed set of the stuff. As Tom had predicted, it began to drizzle, before turning into a heavy fine rain that constantly fell from a leaden overcast sky. There was no doubt about it. The rain was set to persist for the rest of the day. It was then Tom yelled out:

'Didn't I tell you it would damn rain? Didn't I tell you?' As the gang sprang into action, scampering up the steel deck ladders that separated the lower hold from the ship's deck, the ship worker shouted down the hold:

'Get covered up. Beams and hatches on. You barge hands give the lighter-man a hand to re-ship the barge beams. Come on. Jump to it. For Christ's sake don't let the sugar get wet. Where's the crane driver and the "top-hand?"'

'The crane driver's already back in his crane cabin; the "top-hand's" somewhere up on the deck,' Tom yelled, as the first of the beams was being raised up off the deck, slewed across the ship's open hatchway, and lowered with a thud into its deck hatchway coupling.

The dockers soon had the ship closed up: the hatch cover tarpaulins laid out over the wooden deck hatches; the steel hatch bars that secured the tarpaulins back inside the metal cleats; the wooden wedges hammered home to secure the tarpaulins; and the deck booby hatch closed and made secure. It was now a case of trying to find somewhere to shelter until the drizzle stopped falling, which obviously wasn't very likely.

Finding shelter on Tilbury Riverside Cargo Jetty was always a problem, since there was not a single shelter from the elements whatsoever for the men working out there, (there were no toilets [except for the river and the ship's scuppers] or washing facilities either). There were places on most ships one could hide-up in, but most ships, British ships especially, closed up all the deck doors and hatchways to prevent dock workers (or anyone else for that matter) from finding a niche in which to shelter in inclement weather.

However, this particular ship was different though. It was a beaten up old passenger liner, that was now converted into a tramp steamer. It was owned and operated by the Yugoslavian government, and it was doing its rounds of British ports, picking up and dropping off small consignments of freight as it went. It was quite possibly doing a bit of spying for the Yugoslavian and Russian governments too, as a secondary sideline. But at Tilbury docks she was taking on board a thousand tons of Tate and Lyle refined white sugar, after which she was due to sail down river to the deep waters of the lower Thames estuary, to load a quantity of ammunition. Yes, ammunition. Don't forget, at the time of this story it was at the height of the "cold war". Yugoslavia was a socialist country enclosed behind what Winston Churchill had described as "The Iron Curtain".

The ship, being an old liner, had several decks. On each deck was a large salon that had been either a dining room or a foyer that had previously been used as a dance hall once the ship was at sea, during her glorious days cruising the seas and oceans of the world. Now, these once elegant rooms were being used as either cargo space, the ship's storerooms, or in the case of one such room, the crew's personal effects and gear store.

Now, it so happened that the door to the crew's personal store room was not locked, and as us dockers, lighter-men and OST clerks converged on it, slowly one by one infiltrating into it, all in trepidation of being discovered and asked to leave. However, to our utter astonishments and joy, no such order was forthcoming.

The old State Room, because that's what it had once been, was in twilight darkness when the men had first entered it. It was made even darker by the rain clouds low overhead that were slowly making their way down between

34

the river's banks. However, soon after we had gained entry into this very large cabin, the ceiling lights came on as if by magic, and one could take in the whole scene. It was, as I have previously indicated, the crew's personal effects and storeroom. For from rope lashings along the sides of the foyer's bulkheads, standing in neat rows, were second hand iron-framed pianos, pieces of furniture, sewing machines and many other artefacts, plus two guitars that rested on piano lids. At the time of this tale, just after the Second World War, many such items could be purchased from second hand furniture shops, or back street auction rooms, for as little as a few pence or a few shillings. Many of the items were damaged, which indicated they had been rescued from bomb-damaged buildings; or even liberated (thieved) from wartime storage rooms.

The ship's crew had obviously been taking advantage of, and purchasing, such bargains, and it wasn't long before one of the dockers had opened a piano's lid and began to run his fingers along the keyboard. This action was repeated again and again, until every piano in the foyer was being played, each one to a different tune. Some of the pianos had keys that were out of tune, due to the need of retuning, but that only added to the charm of the musical concoction. Some of the dockers began tapping away with bits of wood, using them like castanets, while another pair playing the guitars (in a jazz accompanying fashion) appeared to be trying to drown out the piano players. The un-orchestrated racket continued for some time, until Tom finally yelled above the crescendo:

'Hold it, hold it, you lot. Let's have some coordination here. You're making such a racket you'll get us thrown out if you keep on like that. Now what we need is a lead pianist who all the rest of you will follow; who'll volunteer?'

'I will,' butted in Bill Brag, one of Tom's barge hands. He then said, 'When we've finished one number all stop playing until I've played a "bar" of the next tune, then I'll count up to three and we'll all begin to play together, got that? Right lads, let's give it a whirl,' and away he went.

This co-ordinated playing soon began to bring the ship's crew into focus, a crew that included several young women. At first they began to clap to the music, but it wasn't long before they began to dance; then the Captain and his wife came out of their cabin and joined in. It was at this juncture that several cases of vodka and beer appeared together with ice and glasses; then after a couple of stiff drinks, Barge Carter, one of the dockers, began to sing in a rich tenor voice to the tunes being pounded out from the pianos, and he was soon backed up by several other dockers singing in complete harmony to such songs as: Old Man River, Old Father Thames, Oh Danny Boy and many other songs, while the pianos played, the dockers and the crew danced, and the vodka and beer bottles slowly emptied but were then miraculously replaced. The rain had stopped falling, but nobody attempted to return to work, and when the dockers, lighter-men and OST clerks left the ship, all the crew turned out to see them off. As Tom went to leave, however, the Captain caught his arm and said to him:

'We're supposed to pull out on tomorrow evening's tide. Will we make it?'

'You will, Captain, if the rain holds off,' said Tom. 'You most certainly will. I promise you.'

On the following evening just as Tom had promised, to the cheers of the dockers who had closed the ship up ready for sea, lighter-men and OST clerks, who were now standing on the Cargo Jetty's Decking, the ship was pulled out into the tideway by two William Watkins steam tugboats and turned round into the last water of a high tide. Then, as her propellers began to turn, thrashing the dirty water of the river Thames, she began to make her way slowly down the river Thames to the deep waters off Southend. She was due to keep her appointment there with the "stevedore powder monkeys from Northfleet", who were to finish loading her with a shipment of NATO Lease-Lend missiles and ammunition; supposedly defence armaments for the Yugoslav army.

Now, Just as an After Thought:

It is interesting for me to note now, all these years after that eventful and thoroughly entertaining "musical interlude" aboard that old tramp liner that so many dockworkers in those far off days could play various types of musical instruments, and sing, too. What's more to the point, they all "played by ear", few if any of them had ever had a music lesson in their lives. Most Londoners in the years just after the Second World War, who lived around bomb sites and derelict condemned houses, in the slum tenements of the docklands, were especially adept at playing musical instruments, pianos in particular. When I asked one old work-mate from London why that was, he simply offered the reason those Londoners, especially in places such as Wapping and Tower Hamlets, which were close communities, and where their village halls were the local public houses. The one thing they enjoyed in common which was free, except for the beer, was music. But that was in the days when poor people made their own entertainment. Before the advent of "canned music" and the nauseating racket now foisted upon us by those "factory noises" churned out by modern day Pop Groups. I ask you. Where have all the musically talented people disappeared to; or perhaps more to the point, why have they disappeared?

Little Hughie, and I (Clerking With an Enigma)

Little Hughie, so called because of his minuscule stature, who I shall refer to henceforth simply as Hughie, was an enigma in London's docklands. That is insofar as he was an OST clerk who was not what anyone would even charitably call "fully mentally stable", nor do I don't think he could really be referred to as being positively barmy. But he was certainly some distance away from being considered as stupid or idiotic. Perhaps, therefore, it would be kinder if I were to refer to Hughie as being, well, rather eccentric or, as The Concise Oxford English Dictionary explains it: irregular; odd-acting; capricious. Yes! That's the adjective that best describes Hughie, capricious. A simple word meaning his mind was guided by whim, instead of logical thought, in what most people would consider to be the normal conventional order of things. Well, that's my interpretation of his odd antics.

Hughie, like most other young men and women of his generation, had only latterly returned from war service. He was therefore not alone in his abnormal eccentricities, suffering from a mental condition known among former military servicemen as being "bomb happy," a mental condition that has latterly become known as "combat stress". It is a trauma that afflicted thousands of his comrades whose nerves and minds had been affected through war service. Hughie, I hasten to add, was far away from being alone in his mental state of ambivalence on his return to "civvies-street".

Hughie was also known in the docklands, as were many other members of the docking fraternity, by their stature, or other physical abnormalities. Hughie's designated title of little is the explanation of his sobriquet, for he could not have stood more than five feet three inches tall in his bare feet; he also had middle-aged spread around his waistline. So, yes. I suppose he could be described as being a little bit on the porky side too, that is dumpy. But he was certainly not obese in the true meaning of the word.

One of Hughie other prominent features was he had large greenish-blue piercing eyes, eyes that were always blood-shot as though he had been crying. This gave his eyes the appearance of being two large pieces of alexandrite that had been punched into his moon shaped face. He wore large, horned rimmed glasses, giving him a somewhat searching, sinister look, as though he was reading one's mind with evil intent. His head was covered with a carpet of dark, wavy hair that was going grey around his neck, and thin and wispy at the crown. He had slightly pixie pointed ears that peeped out from under the grey hair similar to listening devices used in undercover surveillance operations. At the time I knew Hughie, he was about thirty or forty something years of age. But as it is for one reason or another with all people of Hughie's mental disorientation, it was impossible without seeing his birth certificate to even hazard a guess as to how old he really was.

However, as I have already explained, Hughie had his odd, eccentric, whimsical ways. For example, during the winter months the little fellow would be seen about the docks wearing cheap plimsolls slippers, (the type sold by Woolworth Stores for a shilling a pair before the Second World War), light trousers, a hand knitted pullover, white open neck shirt and sports jacket. In the summer time he would come to work in the docks wearing Wellington boots, heavy woollen trousers, a hooded anorak jacket; or, depending on the weather, a coat under his oilskins. In other words he would be dressed more like a North Sea trawler-man, than a registered OST ships clerk.

Now you, the reader, may find it extraordinary to learn that just nobody in the docklands ever made fun or made derogatory remarks about Hughie. There was, however, a very good reason for that. The fact of the matter was that before the Second World War Hughie had been employed as a staff charge clerk with a major dock stevedore contractor. Then, soon after the outbreak of war in September 1939, Hughie had volunteered for military service with the British army. He had served, it was said, as a confidential clerk to some high-ranking officer in the Intelligence Corps. Rumour in the docks had been put about, that at the end of hostilities in Europe on 8th May 1945, when the German armies in Europe surrendered to Field Marshall Montgomery (1887-1976) at his Headquarters on Lunenburg Heath. (See Liddell Hart's History of the Second World War, P710, published by Pan Books Limited, 1999). Instead of Hughie being demobilised with his classified army group, he was retained by British Army Intelligence, to act as one of the recording clerks at the Nuremberg War Trials.

The War trials of leading German politicians and military leaders, at which twenty-four of the top Nazi were tried by an international military tribunal consisting of four judges and four prosecutors: these being one judge each from the major victorious nations. Those being the UK, USA, USSR and France, who accused the German cabinet, the general staff, the high command, the Nazi leadership corps, the SS Abteilung and the Gestapo, of criminal responsibility. But who also raised at the war trials blood-chilling facts relating to the ill-treatment, torturing, execution and extermination of millions of prisoners of war (mainly Russians and other Eastern Europeans) in prison camps. Russian civilians—men, women and children, were shot out of hand in their villages, towns and cities whilst Jews, Gypsies, trade unionists, and many other non-conformist groups, were exterminated in gas chambers in concentration camps sited in Poland and Germany itself.

The grizzly facts about the methods used during the Nazi extermination, the "final solution" programme that was brought to light during the Nuremberg Trials, were said to have been the cause of Hughie having a nervous breakdown. A mental breakdown from which he had obviously never fully recovered; and although Hughie had volunteered for Army service, under legislation then currently in force, the dock stevedore contractor by whom he had been previously employed, was duty bound to re-employ him. He therefore returned to the docks, first in his old capacity as a charge clerk, before being demoted to office clerk when his deteriorated mental state became apparent. Then, as a God sent opportunity to his employer, the Dock Workers (Regulation of Employment) Act was introduced in June 1946. Hughie was then transferred out of his permanent job, onto the OST clerks register with the National/London Dock Labour Board, so that whatever untoward clerical errors he may have made in the future could be shared equally with all other port employers of OST clerks.

Of course the other OST clerks and dockers, with whom Hughie worked, looked after him. He was, to be quite blunt about it, embraced within a "brother-hood" which looked after its own; ex-service men who understood Hughie's problem, many from their own bitter personal experiences, far better than any psychologist or psychoanalyst ever could. Hughie was "untouchable" within the docklands fraternity.

There were, of course, other facets to Hughie's post-Nuremberg, post-war characteristics. He never ever did anything in a logical sequence, whilst carrying out his OST clerical duties. That was a fact I was to find out when I was allocated to work with him as his docker/checker, on a loading West African Overseas Trader, where the conventional procedure for OST clerks was as follows:

The OST clerk was in charge of all clerical work appertaining to the ship's hatch he was allocated to. His task was to record all marks, numbers, and measurements of each item of cargo shipped, and to record down which hatch and into which deck the export cargo was being stowed. All exporters' marks, item weights, measurements (to the nearest inch), and numbers were recorded in duplicate. Every item of cargo that was loaded aboard a ship was recorded onto a company's own official "shipping off-loading pad." On the other-hand, a docker/checker's job was to call out the mark, item weight, and number of each individual package, for the OST clerk to record, and to measure each package with a *yardstick* that incidentally was four feet in length, or as in the now accepted European standard measurement, 122cm.

Hughie however, wasn't a conventional OST clerk. He worked differently from any normal run of the mill OST clerk. For example, instead of writing from left to right, or from top to bottom, when recording marks and numbers, he would take the tedium from the job by sometimes working from right to left, or from bottom to top of the marks and numbers. Then, just to confuse one even more, he'd sometimes start in the centre of the marks and numbers, and work his way outwards—what's more he could keep this unique method of his up all day. To say the least, it was an intriguing phenomenon; quite a phenomenal achievement for someone most of his colleagues thought to be, if they were honest about it, quite barmy.

Now it so happened that on the day I'd been allocated to work with Hughie as his docker/checker, I had also been ordered (as a dock shop steward) to attend a meeting in London. So reluctantly I'd asked Hughie if he could manage the job without me. I'd told him, 'One of the docker "pitch hands" will give you a hand as your auxiliary clerk if you should require it.' Hughie just nodded his head.

Oh yes! I forgot to mention another problem one encountered whilst working with Hughie, that was that he never spoke; but the nod of his head was as good an indication I was ever likely to receive from him, that I could go off to my meeting. When I left Hughie, it was with some misgivings that he could get on with his job without me, but I was sure the dockers would keep an eye on him, and give him all the help he may need, after I'd explained to them about my Dock Shop Steward mission to London.

Unfortunately it so happened that one of the OST clerks, Allan B. by name, who was working with the loading gang at the ship's hatch adjacent to Hughie's, had procured a bottle of Scotch whiskey (or two). Allan B., to be blunt about it, was well known throughout the docklands as an alcoholic. There was possibly a fair enough reason for his unfortunate condition; before he had become an OST clerk he had been a merchant seaman, then a docker, before his transfer onto the OST Clerical Register.

Allan had gone to sea at the age of fourteen, and was still quite young when, during the 1939-45 war, he was taken prisoner with other members of his ship's crew, by the German surface raider *Admiral Graf Spee* in the South Atlantic, together with the crews of a number of other ships that had been sunk by Admiral Graf Spee. Allan had been imprisoned on the German supply tanker, *Altmark*. However, soon after Admiral Graf Spee had been cornered by the Royal Naval cruisers, Ajax, Exeter and Achilles, in the River Plate in December 1939, Hitler gave orders to her captain to scuttle Admiral Graf Spee. The Altmark had then re-crossed the Atlantic and was being escorted by Norwegian naval vessels into Jossingfjord, where HMS Cossack caught up with her. Cossack had then followed Altmark into Jossingfjord and forced her to ground. Royal Naval sailors had boarded her, and after some hand-to-hand fighting with bayonets, Altmark's prisoners were released. They were taken aboard HMS Cossack and returned home to Britain, where they once again had to take their chances in the cruel war that was being waged at sea.

Allan B., like all his contemporaries in the Merchant Navy and Armed Services, who had had similar experiences, hardly ever spoke about them. They just lost themselves under the influence of drink to belay their memories, but as was their way they had the knack of inducing others who had had similar experiences to share in the brain reducing pain

45

of such bitter memories through alcoholic intoxication. That is until cirrhosis of the liver did for them what the King's enemies had failed to do during the six years of war while they were fighting at sea, on land or in the air. It slowly killed them off one by one.

When I returned to my job from the meeting in London, I found Hughie standing by a packing case. He was grasping it with both hands, staring straight in front of him, obviously afraid to move. Two of the dockers had taken over Hughie's and my clerical jobs. One was doing the writing, while the other called out the marks and numbers, and fumbled about as he attempted to measure the packages of cargo. They both had that angelic look on their faces, as though they were two of God's chosen people. But their eyes, which looked like a couple of glazed cherries taken off the top of a Dundee cake, gave the pair of those semi-inebriated sots away. For it was quite obvious they had both had a dram or two out of a whiskey bottle themselves.

'What's happened to him?' I asked them, pointing to Hughie.

Neither of them spoke at first, but they then pointed at another figure laying among the cargo, then one of them said with a slur in his voice, 'Pissed as newts they are, the pair of 'em. It's a bloody disgrace, it is, when blokes can't hold their drink.' Then they both burst out laughing.

'You pair of sots,' I admonished them, 'poor bloody Hughie doesn't know what day of the week it is without being drunk. What am I supposed to do with him?'

'He's your mate,' one of them said, giggling like a schoolgirl. 'He's your problem now. Anyway we're just knocking off work for the day. The ship's gang are covering up the lower "'tween deck". Then without so much as a

46

goodbye, or a fare-you-well, they got on their dilapidated bicycles, and rode off along the quay in perfect harmony, swaying from side to side across the railway lines set between the quay cranes, until the front wheels of their cycles got caught between the rails. I'd just turned my back when I heard the crash. I didn't bother to look round. They weren't much good at riding bicycles when they were sober, it was obvious they were even worse at it when they were drunk.

Hughie was holding onto the packing case as though his very life depended on it. I made my way out of the transit shed to a caravan that served as the Clerical Mobile Office for the ship we were loading. Fortunately, the ship's charge clerk was still in residence. I told him of my problem.

'I'd better come and see what I can do,' he said, and followed me along the quay into the transit shed. Hughie was still holding on to the packing case, standing like a miniature statue that reminded me of Eros in Piccadilly Circus.

'Holy Mary!' said the charge clerk, 'How long has he been standing there like that?'

I pointed to Allan, the other OST clerk lying among the cargo, 'I would say about as long as him, I should think.'

'Oh my God,' he gasped. 'Not another one! Give me a hand to get them out onto the quay before the PLA shed man locks the pair of them in for the night.'

We lifted Allan up under his shoulders, dragging him more than carrying him out of the transit shed. We left him slumped up against the transit shed wall, on the quay. He was a big man, weighing something like sixteen stone, no lightweight to drag about. Then we went back to get Hughie, just as the Port Authority shed man came to lock the transit shed doors. We gripped him under the armpits in the same

47

way as we had Allan. He was only half the size and weight of Allan, so we were able to lift him out onto the quay. That's where I let go of him. He instantly grabbed onto the charge clerk's wrists with both hands, gripping him with such power that the charge clerk couldn't break free. The last I saw of them, as I walked off to catch my train, was the pair of them gingerly progressing along the quay towards the Mobile Clerical Office, while Allan lay prostrate against the transit shed, oblivious to this cruel world, and all those bitter memories of his experiences in it.

The last I heard about Little Hughie's antics at work in the London Docklands, was that he'd been in the Dock Labour Board Compound when OST clerks and dockers were being allocated to jobs up-river to the King George V., and the Royal Albert Docks; while a number of other OST clerks and dockers were being sent down-river, off Shell Haven, to load dynamite, detonators, and small arms ammunition.

Hughie had actually been allocated to work in the Royal Albert Docks, but it appears he had decided that a sea trip on an attending Watkins tug would make a nice change from working in the enclosed docks up-river. He therefore made his way with the rest of the men to Tilbury Riverside Landing Stage, and with the down river allocated dockers and clerks he caught a tugboat with those ships gangs allocated to load explosives and ammunition, in a deep-water anchorage in the lower Thames estuary.

However, as Hughie had been allocated to work with a gang sent to the Royal Albert Docks, but had failed to report, the other OST clerks thinking he had lost his way booked him in as though he was in attendance. On the following Thursday, pay day, the Dock Labour Board's wages clerk queried why Hughie had been paid two days' pay for the same day. The OST clerks Trade Union representative was sent for, and was informed of the Dock Labour Board's wages clerk's dilemma. But the TU Officer pointed out that the employing shipping company in the Royal Albert Docks had paid for Hughie's services for that day. He therefore advised the wages clerk Hughie should receive the two days' pay due to him. For as the TU Officer pointed out, technically Hughie had been attending both jobs at the same time, and as his colleagues had carried him for that day, he was entitled to receive both days' payments. Believe me, just nobody else in the London Docklands but Little Hughie, could ever have got away with that. I have to repeat it. Just nobody.

A Yo-Yo Heavy Lift Job (Two Cranes Working in Unison)

The Dock Labour Board Manager came rushing out of his office, heading towards me like a mad bull charging at a Spanish matador. He was waving my attendance book, and a railway warrant in front of him. It was as though he was emulating a frustrated tourist in China during a heat wave, fanning himself ferociously, while suffering from a severe bout of heat stroke. In point of fact, he was in a raging temper, for reasons he never made me privy to, but now there was little reason to believe the object of his present aggressive condition was anyone other than my good self, as I was the only man left in the Dock Labour Compound. Under normal "wage slave" employment conditions, I should have been called to the "labour allocation window" to get my inter-port work orders but on this auspicious day the manager was in one of his usual scarlet moods, that is overbearing, bloody minded and vindictive. He came out of his office door, heading towards me under full steam, with menace in his eyes, venom in his voice, and an enraged look on his fat face. In other words he was his normal obnoxious, bulling self, a pig of a man:

'Right,' he began, snorting at me. Well, they were loud pig-like grunts really, 'you're the only damn crane driver I've got left in the compound. I've been ordered to send my best crane driver that's available to the King George V dock for a special job, you'll have to do because you're the only crane driver I've got. Here's your attendance book and railway warrant, get going.' He then thrust the two documents into my reluctant outstretched hand, then he stood watching me as I hastily made my way out of the dock labour compound. He followed me to the compound door and watched me as I made my way out through the wicket gate, into The Old Dock Road.

Actually, I was the only crane driver left in the compound. There were three reasons for this. The first reason being that as I was a crane driver, I was expected to be competent to do any job in the docks, from driving quay cranes (electric and hydraulic), ships winches (electric and steam) or doing physical labour in a ship's hold, or with some quayside gang. In fact, any job I was called on to perform as a category 'A' crane driver/winch driver or docker. The second reason was that experienced Dock Labour Board managers always held on to their "key-men" for just such an occasion as this; and the Dock Labour Board manager in our Dock Labour Compound, although a vindictive, nasty, *fatherless*, self-opinionated ex-stevedore, he knew about all the vagaries associated in dock working practices, and he was probably enraged at his own stupidity in failing to keep back one of his proven competent crane drivers. The third reason was I had only recently finished my crane driver's training, and passed my test as a crane driver, a grade commonly referred to in the docking industry as a greenhorn. Otherwise, had I been an experienced crane driver, I should have been snapped up to work with a local dock ship's discharging or loading gang, or even a quay delivery gang. So to be absolutely honest about it—local dock ship workers and quay foremen, preferred that greenhorns like me should go and get our mechanical appliance experience, killing or injuring docker workers in other docks, before letting us loose to hawk our limited skills in the docks, where they were responsible for the men in their charge.

Having received my verbal orders, in typical Dock Labour Board management style, I strode out of the Dock Labour Compound, as I have described above, and made my way along The Old Dock Road to Tilbury Town railway station. There I met "No Neck, son of One Arm". (No-Neck was an OST clerk who had been detailed to report to the Blue Star Line Offices in the Royal Albert Docks. He was known as No-Neck because his head rested directly on his shoulders, as though he had dived into the shallow end of a swimming pool that had little water in it, and the force of the impact had shoved his neck down into his chest cavity. No Neck's father had one arm; the other arm was said to have been shot off by a German sniper in the First World War, when he had served as an infantryman in the trenches on the Western Front in Belgium. So that's how father and son were lumbered with the monikers that everyone in the docks knew them by. That was "No Neck, son of One Arm" or "One Arm–No-Neck's old man".

However, whereas No-Arm was a miserable old devil, who took verbal liberties with the dockers, surely knowing full well none of them was going to take advantage of a one armed man, though on several occasions he was challenged to put up a fist, while his erstwhile opponents offered to put one hand behind their back. But such threats never ever came to anything, because One-Arm was in his late sixties or early seventies. Therefore no man would dare to lose face by taking advantage of the old sot. So they would just laugh and say something like:

'We give you best One-Arm. We don't know what you've got hidden up your other sleeve,' or words to that effect. One-Arm would then come out and say something like (and I'm sure he actually believed what he said): 'Yer! I thought you'd back down. Yer haven't got the bottle for it, have yer?' Then he'd take off his spectacles, breathe on the lenses, wipe them with his handkerchief, put them back and straighten them on his nose, pick up his "tally pad", tuck it under the stump of his arm, and get on with doing his job of checking cargo as though nothing had happened. He was a belligerent old sot if ever there was one.

No Neck on the other hand, was a genial, genteel fellow, with a good sense of humour. He was also a devout Catholic, and did a lot of work for his local church. On the journey to Plaistow station from Tilbury Town, No Neck kept me entertained with stories about the Father's antics with his parishioners, the work he himself did for local youth clubs, for the elderly, the disabled, and sick church members. He especially focused on the problem of raising funds, explaining to me the various means of extracting money for this purpose. These ranged from raffles to weekly lottery ticket sales, with bingo in the church hall, and fines for those of the faith who failed to attend the Eucharist on Sundays. So, well before we had reached our destination, No Neck had convinced me of his sincerity, and of the deep attachment he had to his Roman Catholic faith.

On reaching Plaistow Railway Station, we parted company. No-Neck took a bus to the Royal Albert Docks, I caught a bus to take me to Silver Town, opposite to the Tate and Lyle sugar processing factory, where the bus conductress told me I could get into the King George V docks through a "Wicket-Gate". A gate that was set in the outer perimeter of the dock's fifteen-foot high-latticed wooden fence, and from where I could get close to the ship I had been allocated to work on. That ship turned out to be a Blue Funnel liner, loading cargo for the Far East. The ship's loading gang were stevedores; therefore, I knew I would be paid off whatever happened that night. Stevedore ship workers invariably paid off dockers as soon as either a four-hour or a full day's work period was completed. Stevedores did not recognise the "continuity rule" that tied dockers to their jobs until a ship was loaded or discharged. (The "continuity rule" was introduced during the 1939-45 war that made it an offence for port workers to leave any job until it had been completed).

On reaching the bus stop at Silver Town, close to the Tate and Lyle sugar-refining factory, I got off the bus and walked into the King George V docks through a Wicket Gate, where I found *My Ship*. It was a Blue Funnel liner that had derricks with a maximum lifting capacity of 5 tons. Parked on the quay, adjacent to Number two hatch, was a Pickford lorry on which was a large wooden case. The case had marked on it its measurements and weight; the weight was 8 tons nett, 8 tons 10 cwt gross. Being somewhat ignorant of the skills and working ways of London stevedores and dockers, I smiled to myself as I thought, "How is this silly lot of sots proposing to get that 8 ton 10 cwt case aboard that ship, with derricks and cranes that only have a 5 ton lifting capability?" I was to find out the answer to that question soon after, when I reported to the ship worker, who was standing at the head of the ship's gangway:

'Are yer the geezer that's been sent up from down river, sonny?'

'Yes,' I replied, 'Tilbury Docks.'

'Took yer time to get 'ere, didn't yer? Where 'ave yer been?'

'I was the last man in Tilbury Docks Labour Compound,' I told him. 'I didn't get my orders until after eight o'clock. I caught the eight twenty five steam train from Tilbury Town to Plaistow via Barking, I then took a bus to Silver Town. I got here as fast as I could.'

'All right, don't go on,' he groaned, 'you're beginning to sound like my old woman. I know the route from Tilbury. Have you reported to the office?'

'No! I came straight here to the ship.'

He looked me up and down then said, 'You're a bit young to be a crane driver, ain't yer? Had any experience working aboard ships, have yer?'

'I'm probably the youngest crane driver in the Port of London,' I boasted, 'and I've spent four years working aboard ships.'

'Well, I hope you're up to doing this Yo-Yo heavy lift job,' he said before continuing. 'You had better go over and report to the office, hand your attendance book in, then come back here. By the time you get back I may have the job that you've come to do, ready for you,' and with those last few words he walked off along the ship's deck towards number two hatch, where the "top-hand" was already busy laying dunnage close by the ship's rail, preparing it ready to take the heavy lift case when it was put aboard the ship.

I went ashore and made my way to the Blue Funnel Line office, where I was bombarded with the same, what I term to be stupid, questions, 'You're late; where have you been?' some pompous ass of an office clerk asked.

By this time I was beginning to get quite angry, 'Would you believe me if I told you on a Puffer Train, an Omnibus and Shanks Pony?' I replied.

'Are you trying to be facetious or downright impertinent?' he snapped.

'Take it whatever way you like,' I told him, 'Don't try throwing your limited vocabulary at me, I'm not in the mood for it. By the way, what time was it this morning you decided to "indent" for a second crane driver for the ship's gang working at Number two hatch?'

But the only reply I got to that question was, 'Go back to the ship,' and the ignorant sot turned his back on me and walked away. (The thing that annoyed me most about that type of individual was that they depended on our dock working skills for their livelihoods, not we on their clerical or organising ability, thank God).

I walked back to the ship, where the ship worker told me when I reached the top of the gangway, 'You'd better go and get yer dinner. I won't need yer until one o'clock. I've got to have a crane shift and finish laying dunnage on the deck at Number two hatch, and the carpenters have got to rig some extra support beams under the upper 'tween deck, to take the extra weight of that case we are going to stow on deck.'

'Where can I go for lunch?' I asked him.

'Lunch? Oh lunch! There's a place just outside the Wicket Gate. It's called George's Café, you'll get a good meal in there, but be back here sharp at one o'clock,' and he walked away towards Number two hold, where the last stage of this dockland drama was to take place.

56

I walked back down the ship's gangway onto the quay, traced my way back to the Wicket Gate, strode back towards the bus stop where I had alighted from the bus that had brought me here, and found George's Café at the corner of a street. It was only a small place, that had about thirty chairs laid out around six or seven tables. The café had just opened when I arrived, and there was only one man seated. It struck me that the ship worker had sold me a "dead pup", if the place was this popular. But I thought I'd get some advice on the quality of the food before I ordered a meal, so I went and sat down opposite the only other customer in the place, an old man who was reading a magazine article on atomic fusion:

'Good morning,' I said. 'I'm sorry to interrupt your perusal of that scientific periodical, but the café's not too busy—is it about to close?'

'Close?' he replied, 'It's just damn well opened.'

'I wondered,' I said, 'only there's no one here except you and I.'

'You're bloody lucky son to get in here, give it another quarter of an hour and this café will be full, and men will be queuing up outside on the pavement.' Then he said, 'Where are you from?'

'Tilbury Docks.'

'That explains your ignorance of this place. Now let me tell you, sonny. This café gives the best service and meals anywhere in London's Docklands. You'd have to go to the Savoy Grill to get better grub than they serve here in George's Café, but it would cost you a bit more there than the half-crown your dinner will cost you here.'

It was then that Mrs George, the proprietor's wife, came to our table and asked if she could take our orders. 'Better do that before the rush starts, Ernie,' she said.

'What's on the menu today, lovely?' my companion asked.

'Steak, chips and peas, or steak pie, mashed potatoes and peas—apple pie or spotted dick with custard for sweet, Ernie,' she said.

Ernie was obviously a regular customer and he replied, 'I'll have the steak pie, mash and peas, with spotted dick and custard for afters,' then he turned to me. 'What do you want?'

'I'll have the same as you, Ernie,' I replied, 'with a mug of tea please.'

Mrs George looked down at me and smiled, then she said to Ernie, 'He's a polite young man. Where's he from?'

'Tilbury Docks.'

'Oh!' she exclaimed, 'That explains it; gentleman docker, not like you coarse lot up here in the smoke.' (The smoke was how Londoners in general referred to their city in those far off days, because of the continuous fogs and smog that pervaded the metropolis in the latter months of each year).

'Carrot Cruncher, more like,' Ernie said with a laugh, as Mrs George walked away. Then he turned towards me and asked, 'Do you live in Tilbury, sonny?'

'No,' I replied, 'I come from Gravesend.'

'So do I, but I now reside in Abbey Wood.'

'Oh!' I said in surprise, 'You're Ernie B., aren't you?'

'Yes I am,' then, 'how did you know that?'

'Well, you're my uncle.'

'Your uncle? Who on God's earth are you?'

'I'm your brother Percy's son.'

'Well,' he said, 'I should have known that by your sheer bloody arrogance.'

I laughed and said, 'I'm as surprised as you, the last time I saw you was when you were demobilised from the army in 1945. How have you been keeping these last ten years?'

'I've only been back to work a few weeks,' he told me. 'I got knocked down a ship's hold.'

'Oh!' I said it in that matter of fact way men working in dangerous industries spoke to each other about such things those days, 'Was there much physical damage?'

'I broke both my legs, but the hospital registrar and orthopaedic surgeon that treated me told me there was no other damage. I told both of them my hip joints were playing me up, but they ignored my complaint, sent me back to work today. But enough about me, what have you been sent here from Tilbury for?'

'To work a Yo-Yo on that Blue Funnel ship lying at thirteen shed. But to be truthful, I've not the slightest idea what a Yo-Yo is, except for the toys we used to get from Woolworth Stores when we were children, that we bounced up and down on a piece of string. Nor do I know what I'm expected to do with a Yo-Yo on a ship, and I've not had the nerve to ask. I thought I just wait and see what I am expected to do.'

'Well, to put your mind at rest, the principal of working a toy Yo-Yo, and crane Yo-Yo is exactly the same. I'd better explain,' my Uncle Ernie said. He then went on to outline the way in which a Yo-Yo was operated between two cranes, to put heavy lift cargoes aboard ships:

'What they'll do is bring two cranes face-to-face on the quay adjacent to the hatch, where the heavy lift is to be stowed for the voyage; then they will place a heavy lift wire over each crane hook that will have a single heavy duty pulley block and tackle wheel on it. The ship's official crane driver will have the job of placing the heavy lift where it is to be stowed on deck. All you have to do is follow his lead. Wherever he goes with his crane jib, you follow with your crane jib, keeping the load evenly balanced between your two jibs. Got that?'

'Yes, I think so,' I said. 'I just follow the other crane driver's lead, wherever he goes with his crane jib, I follow with my crane jib, keeping the load evenly balanced.'

'That's right,' he confirmed, and he went silent while we each ate our lunch.

We sat for some time after having eaten our lunch, talking. My uncle explaining, or more to the point lecturing me, on the dangers of uncontrolled nuclear bomb testing. He explained to me what results would accrue from the effects of radioactive dust, when it was spewed into the atmosphere after every test explosion. That it was his opinion it would result in thousands, if not millions of deaths around the world in the future from cancer. I must admit the enormity of the effect of radioactive fallout on future generations of the human race, due to political naivety of the dangers inherent in the new science of atomic energy, and the jingoistic ranting of Eastern and Western block politicians, as to which corrupt political system was best suited to their own benefit, was over shadowed by my need to understand the rudimentary principles of getting a heavy lift packing case aboard a Blue Funnel liner, using a Yo-Yo. So I have to admit I took my leave of Uncle Ernie, (that was the last time I ever saw him), paid my half-crown for the scrumptious George's Café lunch, and made my way back to the Blue

Funnel liner ready to put Uncle Ernie's instruction on the use of a two crane Yo-Yo into practice.

As I approached the ship, I noticed she was flying a Blue Peter flag, (a Blue Peter is a flag with a blue background and a white square in its centre. It is hoisted to the top of a ship's mast as a signal the vessel is ready to sail) so she was obviously due to be floated out of the docks to catch the top of the next ebbing tide. When I arrived on the quay, I noticed there were four Stothard and Pitt eighty foot jibed quay cranes shunted up close together, two three ton lift cranes in between two five ton lift cranes. What was more, all the other ship's hatches had closed down, as their cranes had been put out of service by the need to get the heavy lift put aboard the ship.

The ship worker and the ship's crane driver were waiting for me on the quay when I got back. Then, as I approached the cranes by the ship's side, the ship worker with the comment, 'You're late back, sonny,' welcomed me.

I looked at my watch and told him, 'It's five to one. I'm not due back to start work until one o'clock.'

The ship worker, without looking at his watch said, 'My watch must be fast. Don't sod me about. I've got to get this ship loaded. You two get up in those cranes. Let's get this show on the road.' The ship's crane driver smiled and winked, but kept silent, as we parted company and clambered up into our respective mechanical contraptions.

When we had each turned on the electric current that fed the cranes motors, we simultaneously lowered our crane hooks, for the stevedore pitch hands on the quay to place the heavy lift wires that held the Yo-Yo in place onto them. Then, when we had raised the Yo-Yo and lifting wires above the packing case, the pitch hands slipped one wire under each end. Then, on the hand signals of the ship's "top hand", we raised the Yo-Yo and began to lift it slowly skywards until it reached just above the ship's rail level. Then the lead crane driver slowly slew his crane jib over to the ship's deck, followed closely by my crane's jib, and on the "top hand's" signal to lower, the heavy lift case was slowly and delicately dropped in place onto the ship's deck. The whole operation took no more than five or ten minutes, and before I had had time to line my crane up with the quay, it was being unceremoniously shunted back to number four ship's hatch, from whence it had been "borrowed" for the stevedore gang working there to continue loading cargo.

When I had climbed out of the crane cabin, and reached the bottom of the crane's three vertical ladders, the ship worker was there to greet me with 'That was a lovely piece of work sonny, a lovely piece of work. Now here's your Attendance Book stamped up for the day. I won't be wanting yer any more today, so off yer go, home.'

The time was about fifteen minutes past one. So I decided that instead of returning to Gravesend by the Tilbury to Gravesend ferry service, via Plaistow, barking and Tilbury riverside stations, I'd catch a bus from silver town to north Woolwich, walk under the river through the tunnel that connects north Woolwich with Greenwich, and take a train to Gravesend from there. I hadn't bothered to look at my attendance book, thinking the Blue Funnel Line would only stamp it up to a 5:00 p.m. work period.

I was in Tilbury Dock Labour Compound the following morning, for the 7:45 a.m. muster. But no ship worker or quay foreman wanted to "pick up" a "green horn" crane driver such as myself. When the "free call" was over, the tannoy system blared out: "All attendance books in". Those

'A' Men that had failed to obtain a job dutifully took their attendance books to the Dock Labour Board Office and passed them through the open office windows to the office clerks; while the genuine category 'C' and 'B' men who had shown up for work, but whose signing-on day it was not, walked out of the compound with long, downcast faces, to try their luck for a job on the morrow. That is with the exception of the taxi drivers, boarding house keepers, and other small time businessmen, that left the Dock Labour Board Compound smiling. After all, they had surreptitiously obtained their 'C' category docker's brief by devious means in order to avoid the Inland Revenue from looking into their "moon-lighting rackets."

After all, it was a devious trick. The Dock Labour Board paid their National Insurance Stamps, and saw to their Income Tax returns for them, paid out of their full back guarantee wages from the monies which were taken out of the wage levy paid by the port employers, based on wages earned by those registered men who were working.

After I had put my attendance book in with those of the rest of the 'A' Men, I stood by myself, leaning against the steel rail that was used to separate the ship workers and quay foremen from the dockers during the period of the 'free call', when I was ordered over the tannoy system to report to the office window. The Dock Labour Board Manager was waiting at a window hatch, holding my attendance book in his hand:

'What,' he demanded to know in his usual obnoxious, pig ignorant manner, 'are you doing at work?'

'Waiting for a job,' I replied.

'Have you looked at your attendance book?' He snorted as he thrust it into my hand.

'No,' I said, 'I finished that job in the King George V dock you sent me to do yesterday, just after one o'clock, Why?'

'Because, you stupid oaf, your attendance book is stamped up for a short night.' (A short night meant I had been paid up until midnight, and had no need to report for work the following day).

Clutching my Attendance Book, and without saying another word, I walked out of the Compound and went home. On the following Thursday, pay day, I got a lovely surprise. Not only had I been paid a 'short night's' money, but also my crane-con for the whole day. I had also been paid pro-rata to the ship's gang's piecework earnings. The Blue Funnel Line ship worker must have been very well pleased with my Yo-Yo performance, a performance for which I must give my late uncle Ernie the full credit.

After that meeting in "George's Café", I never met my uncle Ernie again. He was forced to leave the docks due to the accident from which he was said to have suffered two broken legs, however, due to the hospital registrar's, and consultant orthopaedic surgeon's recommended treatment, and contrary to their expert opinions as to the severity of his injuries. Injuries it was later discovered by X-rays at the Manor House Hospital included fractures of the lower spine and crushed coccyx. Both of uncle Ernie's hips had been damaged, and although both his hips were replaced, my uncle Ernie was condemned to spend the rest of his life in a wheelchair. So that was that.

The Lottery Club Fiddlers(The Dockers Clubs Social Committee)

George, the esteemed down hold foreman of our dockers ship's gang, was in earnest conversation with Dolly, a Port of London Authority "mobile tea lady". Dolly's hands were waving about in the air, like a pair of newly washed gloves hanging on a washing line that was blowing about in a gale force wind. George's head, on the other hand (that's a pun), was nodding up and down in such a way as to remind one of the nodding donkeys on an oilfield well-head site. Oddly enough though, the pair of them must have been talking in whispers, because except for George's head nodding, and Dolly's hand waving, not a sound of their voices could be heard. Believe me it wasn't because the rest of us members of George's gang weren't trying our best to impinge on the gist of their apparent harangue discourse. It was as frustrating as watching a married couple rowing in a silent film—but without the benefit of underwritten sub-titles.

We, our ship's gang that is, hadn't had a job for several weeks, even though we had been reporting for work twice each day (7:45 a.m. and 12:45 p.m.) at Sector 3, Tilbury Docks Dock Labour Compound Office, of the London Dock Labour Board. (The Labour Compound was the pick-up point for dockers seeking work. It was a place more commonly known to us dockers as "the dockers' dole house").

This ritual of hawking our bodies (like prostitutes or rent boys), in exchange for work and money payments, had been going on each day from Monday to Friday, and once on Saturday morning, day in and day out. This was the case for most of the dockers attached to Sector 3, Tilbury Dock Labour Compound, as we waited with growing impatience and anxiety for ships to enter the empty docks complex, for there was now a wide gap in the "liner passenger/cargo shipping schedules" of both the Orient Line and Pacific and Orient Line fleets of vessels. Ocean cargo/passenger liners were the main stay of employment in Tilbury docks. For these ships plied their trade on the high seas between Tilbury Docks, in the Port of London, and the Australian seaports of Brisbane, Sydney, Melbourne, Adelaide and Perth. In fact there were almost as many ocean cargo/passenger liners sailing to Australasian sea ports, as there were deep-sea overseas traders operating the sea routes between the Port of London, the Indian sub-continent, Ceylon, and the Far Eastern ports of Rangoon, Singapore and Hong-Kong.

The reason for this tragedy was due to the Suez Canal, an international waterway previously owned by the British and French Governments, having been nationalised then blocked by the Egyptian Government in 1956. It was a situation that caused shipping companies to divert luxury passenger/cargo carrying liners, and cargo carrying liners, away from the Mediterranean and Suez Canal route to India, Far East and Australasian countries. The passenger/cargo liners thereafter crossed the Atlantic Ocean to New York, sailed through the Panama Canal and crossed the Pacific Ocean to begin trading from the Australian western port of

Perth. It was a sea route that added an extra month to the passenger liner/cargo ships sailing schedules of Orient Line and Pacific and Orient Line ships.

On the other hand, the cargo liners, and tramp steamers, on which we Tilbury dockers also depended for our livelihoods, had to be diverted down the Atlantic coast of West Africa into the Southern Ocean, round the Cape of Good Hope into the Indian Ocean, and sail up the East African coast across the Arabian Sea to India and other Far Eastern countries to trade. They were journeys that took trading ships many extra weeks to complete, over and above the normal shipping schedules; a costly and time consuming exercise for everyone involved in both the shipping, and port transport industries.

Therefore, except for the odd Brocklebank, City Line and Clan Line cargo boats that sailed into the docks with a few thousand chests of tea and a few hundred tons of cases of carbon black, bales of gunnies, bags of maggoty bones, or a deck cargo of live animals such as elephants, caged tigers, and other such imports from India and other Near East countries, had remained almost 'moth-balled' for weeks. The dockers employed in Sector 3 Tilbury docks were becoming increasingly despondent by the lack of work, loss of wage income, and nagging desperate wives. Most of those men that had 'dabbed on' had gone off scavenging for whatever they could lay their hands on. All of those, that is, except the taxi cab drivers, guest house, boarding house and corner shop keepers, who had falsely obtained a "dockers or stevedores" Dock Workers Registration through their church, Masonic Lodge or other such organisation, and had got themselves medically down-graded as category 'C' men through the same connections, so they could go about their true vocations without having to worry about declaring their "black economy earnings" to the Inland Revenue, or of having to purchase "self-employed" National Insurance Stamps.

'C' men were meant to be men with recognised serious industrial injuries or diseases. Men who had been medically downgraded as unfit to perform all those employment duties required of dockers and stevedores under the Dock Workers (Regulation of Employment) Act, 1946. However, category 'C' men were obliged to report for work three days each week, for which they received 6/11ths of the "fall back guarantee". This payment was the most they were permitted to receive, even though they may have attended all eleven calls in any one week in the hope of getting at least one day's work.

On the days of this particular tale however, our ships gang had managed to get a job delivering tea chests onto lorries. The work was boring and monotonous, with long breaks between vehicles turning up to be loaded. So we sat about on chests of tea, while we waited for the lorry transport to turn up. During these tedious breaks, some of the men played cards, while others sat and talked about their hobbies, or their view on the political situation; a couple of them sat reading the sports section in newspapers while Terry, our workmate with academic qualifications and intellectual reasoning powers, that I sometimes found were far beyond my ability to understand, sat apart from all of us, reading the Daily Worker (or was it the Morning Star?). He always sat alone when we weren't working, engrossed in his own thoughts. Now it was 9:30 a.m.; "Beer Ho" time; and the 'mobile canteen' had turned up on the quay.

Dolly, the mobile tea lady, helped by a couple of dockers, opened the "mobile tea hut" that stood adjacent to the transit shed, lifted the wooden flap that revealed a counter onto which she organised tea and coffee urns, and trays of meat, cheese, and beef dripping sandwiches, meat and cheese rolls, cakes and bread pudding, from which she served the working gangs, OST clerks, lighter-men and lorry drivers with victuals.

It was soon after Dolly had finished serving the men that she and George had got into their intense conversation, the subject matter of which up to that moment in time, us other members of his gang had not the slightest notion of. However, after Dolly and George had broken into their hand waving—head nodding conversation of the uttermost intensity, it became obvious to all of us that something very serious was being discussed, so we went back into the transit shed to await George's return.

George came back into the transit shed with his head bent forward, and his hands raised up towards his shoulders, as though he was Atlas carrying the world on his broad back. Bert, our former pugnacious barge hand, who had become George's firm friend since an altercation over a game of cards said: 'OK George, what was that chin-wagging, hand waving, head nodding conversation all about then, old mate?'

'The Club Lottery Bert,' George replied. 'Dolly was saying it was crooked, because nearly every week someone on the club committee, or one of their relatives, wins the "jack-pot" and so they do when you come to think about it.'

'Don't be stupid,' said Brains, the gang's only non-thinking member with a mental blockage equivalent to a tight cork in a wine bottle (or a Member of Parliament filing through the House of Commons lobby, at the behest of his political party's whips, to vote on a government policy issue the consequences of which he doesn't understand). 'No one could find a way of fiddling *Our Club Lottery*.'

'Our club lottery!' George replied. Then how is it that nearly every week one of the club committee members, or one of the committee members' family, wins the "jackpot"?'

'Because they must buy more tickets between them than anyone else, you stupid sot,' said Brains.

George spun round and let fly a vicious right hook to Brains' jaw that was only stopped by Bert taking the full weight of the blow in the palm of his hand.

'Leave it, George,' Bert said, 'you're wasting your time. He's too thick to even work out what one and one add up to.'

'Yes, that and the fact Jim D., the Club Committee's Secretary, is his father-in law,' Charlie, another of the gang members, interjected.

'Is he by Jesus!' replied George.

The discussion raged on for some time, as individual gang members put forward their separate ideas as to how the Dockers' Lottery could be fiddled, and to the counter arguments that dismissed the whole idea that it was possible to fiddle the system. After all, a couple of the gang argued, how could anyone separate the four winning numbers from fifty balls that were spun in a drum; especially as a different member of the Lottery Club Committee was nominated to extract four stone balls from the rotated drum each week.

The lottery was a simple system, run on the basis that committee members sold books of tickets at five shillings a book, (twenty five new pence). Each book contained twenty tickets that were numbered; the ticket numbers ran from one up to fifty. The prize draw was made every Friday evening in the Club House. The way the winning numbers were obtained was that a committee member was asked, on a rota basis, to take five balls from a drum that held fifty numbered small stone balls. After each single ball was removed from the drum, a handle attached to the drum was turned to give the watching club members the impression the stone balls were being shuffled. After four balls had been removed from the drum, they were placed in order of value on a raised stand. It was then the holder of those numbers on a single ticket, who was decreed to be the winner of that week's lottery prize. A supposedly fool proof system?

Terry sat looking at his Daily Worker (or was it The Morning Star?), not reading it but obviously deep in thought, saying nothing, just shaking his head in disbelief, but smiling and keeping his thoughts to himself.

'What's so damn funny, Terry?' George asked him, 'We're all being taken for a ride if what Dolly suspects about the Club Lottery is true.'

'Not all of us, George,' replied Terry, 'for neither Bert nor I gamble, so we don't get turned over by those petty shysters that run the Club Lottery. I've been listening to your various arguments and theories on how the *fiddle* is carried out, and to those arguments that state it's not possible to cheat the system. But for your information and edification, there's not been a system invented yet that can't be overcome by human ingenuity. If a human being can invent it, then a human being can break it.'

'So what has that brilliant intellectual mind of yours deduced from our discussions?' said Brains, whose somewhat minuscule mental capability was obviously functioning far beyond its normal design stage, 'What's the answer? Is the Lottery being fiddled or isn't it? And if it is, how is it being done?'

Terry roared with laughter and said, 'Of course it's being fiddled. There's nothing on this earth that can't be fiddled. Now one of you give an example of something you think can't be cheated, and I'll give you a counter to your argument that will prove you to be wrong.'

'What about that University Challenge programme on television?' One of the gang members suggested. 'How could the programme organisers fiddle that?'

'Now that's a good example of how cheating can be done,' replied Terry. 'It's one of the simplest systems because it can be done with impunity, and most people would be none the wiser.'

'How is that possible?' said Bert.

'Because,' Terry replied, 'two teams of university students are selected to face each other at any one time. In order to give one university team the edge over another, the organisers simply, by having prior knowledge of the prime subjects of the colleges taking part, could manipulate the course of questions to suit whatever university college they chose to win,' then he added, 'I'm not suggesting it ever has been done; but it is possible to do it.'

Brains, who was sitting on a tea chest, thoughtfully stroking his stubbly whiskered chin, then said, 'What do you mean by subject matter?'

All the heads of the other gang members, turned towards Brains in disbelief. Charlie barked out: 'You putty brained bloody idiot,' but Terry held up his hand and stopped any further verbal abuse by continuing:

'That's not a silly question at all because it gets to the gist of how the scam that I'm explaining to you could happen. Now let's assume the producer, or the programme's researchers, were of a mind to see a particular university win the University Challenge Competition. As examples, take the Oxbridge Colleges, because they are renowned for producing academics. A goodly number of Oxbridge graduates go on to become top ranking civil servants, especially in the Foreign and Colonial Offices. Now supposing one of the Oxbridge colleges was drawn against a team of students from the London School of Economics and Political Science (LSE), where the main subjects are social sciences. It is easy enough to rig the lead question towards arts that, if the Oxbridge team are up on their subjects, they must win more of the prime questions. It doesn't matter that they may falter with answering most of the bonus questions; they must win the contest. Of course, the same applies if the LSE is scheduled for a win, then economic and other social science questions shall dominate the prime questions asked by the Question Master.'

'What happens if the biased questions being asked are challenged?' Bert asked.

'That's never going to happen,' Terry replied, 'because the programme's producer and the researchers are considered to be beyond reproach. However, there can always be an upset, especially if one in either team already has a degree that covers the prime questions, but that is only likely to happen if a mature student who, unknown to the programme producer, already has an university degree that covers the prime questions.'

'Are there many examples where a system has been penetrated by devious means, Terry?' George asked.

'Loads of them, I don't doubt,' Terry replied.

'Right, give us a for instance,' said George.

Terry sat for a few moments, strumming his lips with his index finger before he replied, then he said: 'I suppose the best example from an electrically operated system was the "Heath Robinson" used in combination with a switchboard-like device known as "Tunny".'

'What the hell are you talking about now?' said Brains, 'Heath Robinson? Sodden Tunny? What's all that got to do with the Club Lottery?'

'Shut your noise, Brains,' said George, 'We want to know what Terry is getting at.'

'Well,' Terry continued, 'during the Second World War the Germans had a machine they called Enigma, it was a machine that sent out coded messages. The Germans thought the codes couldn't be broken by cryptanalysts, because the German signallers changed the sprockets each day before sending messages. The obvious object of this exercise was to confuse international code breakers. However, unbeknown to the German military hierarchy, two Polish scientists stole one of the Enigma coding machines and brought it to Britain. The consequence of the British obtaining an Enigma machine was that a large code breaking team of professional cryptanalysts (egg-heads) from universities, and even "crossword puzzle solvers" were assembled at a place called Bletchley Park. To give you some idea of the importance attached to this operation, it is estimated that over eight thousand top-notch brains were said to have been employed, working on this code breaking operation.'

'You're having us on, Terry,' said Charlie. 'Eight thousand brains in one place, trying to solve problems that came from a German coding machine?'

'Yes, Charlie,' said Terry, 'Straight up, but what a machine! Enigma machines were sending out cipher traffic at the rate of over ten thousand messages a day. Then, in 1942, the German High Admiral Donitz realised his naval Enigma codes were being deciphered. So he ordered an increase to be made in the number of sprockets on their maritime Enigmas, with the consequence that the whole of the British North Atlantic Fleet were without Naval Intelligence as to the German U-boat strategy in the North Atlantic ocean.'

'Just like a sodden Jerry, kicking the ball out of play when we were heading for goal; but what's that got to do with "fiddling" the club lottery?' Charlie insisted. Then he said, 'Now where did you say the Germans were playing football in the North Atlantic? I was serving on a destroyer in the North Atlantic on convoy duty during the war. I didn't see any Germans playing football,' Charlie joked.

'Damn you, Charlie,' said George, 'It's idiots like you that get us dockers a bad name. Now, what did the "egg-heads" at Bletchley Park do to overcome this new problem, Terry?'

'Well,' Terry replied, 'there was a bloke at Bletchley Park. Well, he was said to have been more of a *blokess* really, because he was said to have been as gay as a traditional Christmas pudding made of sponge cake mixture. But he was by all accounts a mathematical genius, a bloke by the name of Alan Turing.'

'Was he one of them *him-she's*, Terry?' Brains said, 'I've heard about them sort before, them is lesbians aren't they?'

'Well, that's one way of putting it, Brains,' Terry replied, 'You're probably getting close with that description, because Turin was known to have been a practising homosexual.'

'What's a homosexual, Terry?'

'The same thing as you've described in sexually disorientated women, but in men,' replied Terry. 'Now, where was I? Oh yes, Turing realised his cryptanalysts were being beaten by those sneaky Germans, who began changing the sprocket ratios on their Enigma machines. So he and his fellow "egg-heads" finally had to denigrate themselves, and approached the Post Office with a request for technical assistance.'

'The Post Office, Terry?' said George. 'What could the Post Office do to help the cryptanalysts, give them its stamp of approval?' It was a remark that brought a roar of laughter from other gang members, and a sullen smirk of disapproval from Terry.

'What's a cryptanalyst, Terry?' Brains asked.

Terry patiently explained, 'They're people that decipher problems; code breakers or crossword puzzle solvers, those sorts of people.'

'Like you when you're doing the Times crossword?' said Brains.

'Yes,' replied Terry, 'exactly like that. It's all about solving problems, in this case an electrically operated code system sent through Enigma coding machines.'

'So how did this Alan Turing finally beat the Enigma coding system, Terry?' Charlie asked.

'I've already told you that, you confounded blockhead. By approaching the Post Office for assistance. The Post Office responded to Turin's request by sending one of its electrical telephone engineers to Bletchley Park, a chap by the name of Thomas Fowler. Now Thomas Fowler was a

Londoner like us, but with a slight difference, he was educated. When he'd graduated from London University, he joined the Dollis Hill research station of the Post Office, and with a number of like-minded colleagues, he was involved in electronic telephone transmission work.'

'Why did Turing and his "egg-head" mates want Fowler at Bletchley Park?' George asked, 'What could this Thomas Fowler do that Turing and his "egg head" mates couldn't do?'

'Well, as I have already explained, Thomas Fowler was an electrical engineer; the Enigma problem was an electrical engineering problem. Thomas Fowler, therefore, in collaboration with Turing, set about building machines that could, and did, decipher the Enigma codes. That's what Thomas Fowler did. One of the machines he built was named the Colossus, and it was used to crack the more complex codes used by the German Enigma-encoded Morse transmissions.'

'I've never heard of Thomas Fowler or this Enigma machine,' said Brains, 'and I read a lot, you know.'

'The closest you come to reading anything of interest, you pigeon-brained numbskull,' said Bert, 'is the Dandy, and Film-Fun comics, and you only do that when you're sitting on the toilet.'

'How'd you know that?' said Brains, to a bout of laughter from the other members of the gang. Bert just shook his head, but said nothing. He knew Brains' mental capability was already overheating, and wouldn't stand too much more thinking pressure before he burst out in a violent rage.

'What happened to the decoding machines Thomas Fowler made, Terry?' Charlie asked.

'Ten of them were broken up on Prime Minister Winston Churchill's orders when the war ended; smashed to fragments for some idiotic reason of his own. Or was it? Only one of them was left, and records show that it was taken to GCHQ at Cheltenham. No doubt that machine was used in the so-called *cold war* against the Russians,' Terry replied.

'What happened to Thomas Fowler?' George asked. 'I'd never heard of him until you mentioned his name.'

'Neither has anyone else, George. When the war was over he returned to work on research at the Dollis Hill Post Office Research Centre. For his major contribution in winning the war, and creating the first workable computer, he was awarded a derisory MBE. I suppose if he'd been a film star, or one of the cryptographers working on the Enigma decoding operations, he may have got a knighthood; unfortunately for him, he was only the electrical engineer who designed and built "the geese that laid the golden eggs". Well, that's how Churchill described his decoding machines.'

'Yes,' said Charlie, 'but what has all this to do with fiddling the Club Lottery?'

'Ah!' said Terry, 'I'm coming to that, because I want you to understand the answer to any problem is to tackle it from the same direction from which it evolves.'

'What! Like a re-examination of a crime scene the police set up when they're investigating a murder?' Brains asked.

'Yes, similar to that. For example in the case of University Challenge, answering the key questions is the crucial factor in winning the contest. In the case of the electronic Enigma machine, creating an electronic computing machine was the only answer to quickly solving the ciphered Enigma messages. But as you have unknowingly explained to me without realising the significance of them, in the case of the Lottery Club Fiddle, it's all to do with the balls.'

'What do you mean by the balls?' said George.

'The balls in the revolving drum,' Terry replied, 'That's where the answer lies to this Lottery Club Fiddle problem.'

'How can you know that?' Charlie asked.

'Simply because the balls in the revolving cylinder are the last items in the equation, or to put it more succinctly, the last piece of the puzzle, they don't stand up to scrutiny. So let's look at the process through which the Club Lottery is run: Obviously the club has to order the lottery tickets from a printer; the tickets are collected and taken to the Club House, where vendors are supplied with X-amount of books. The books of tickets are then sold on to club members and others, the money from the sales is returned to the Club Secretary. The total cash takings from that week's ticket sales are then counted, and after the Club Treasurer has taken ten or twenty percent from the overall total income for club funds, the remainder of the cash is then allocated as prize money. So now we come to the question. How is it possible to fiddle the system?'

'That's what we keep asking you,' said George. 'Now stop sodden us about. How do those committee shysters fiddle the system so they win most of the lottery prize money each week?'

'Well now, I'll tell you how I think it's done,' said Terry. 'First the committee members select a book of tickets that hold the winning number. Then whichever committee member's turn it is to win that week, he is sold what will be the book with the winning ticket.'

'Don't take us for a load of fools, Terry,' said Charlie. 'How can one of the committee members be sold the winning ticket, if the draw hasn't taken place?'

'But don't you see, Charlie? The draw has already taken place, because the winning ticket has been sold. The only thing that has to happen now to legitimise the winning ticket, is for those stone balls in the drum with numbers that coincide with the chosen ticket numbers, have to be taken from the drum on the night of the Club Lottery Draw.'

'Right, so how do the committee members arrange that, Terry?'

'Well, my theory is that on the night before the lottery draw, possibly when they select the book with the winning ticket number, the committee members remove the four stone balls whose numbers are the same as those on that ticket selected to win the lottery prize that week; they are then put to one side. Now the Club House room temperature is always kept at a comfortable level, say about 15 degrees centigrade, in other words it's always warm, which means the numbered stone balls left in the drum are at room temperature. Now I don't normally bet, but I'll bet you any money you like, that the Club Committee has a refrigerator in the Committee Room where they keep their personal beer supplies and other perks. And I bet you too, that the infamous drum in which *all* the stone balls are kept are generally housed in the Committee Room, near to a warm radiator, until it's taken out into the main hall on the night of the Lottery Draw. I said *all*, but in fact there are only forty six balls in the drum.'

'No, Terry, there's fifty balls in the drum,' said Brains.

'I've just told you there are forty six balls in the drum, Brains,' said Terry.

'OK, Terry, so where are the other four balls?' Bert asked.

'For my money, if I was a betting man, I'd say they'll be in the refrigerator,' Terry replied.

'So what are they doing in the refrigerator?'

'Freezing, I wouldn't wonder,' said Terry laughing.

'Why's that?' said Brains as he scratched his head.

'I'll explain that to you later, after we've won the lottery,' said Terry. Then he continued by asking Bert, 'Doesn't your wife do a bit of cleaning in the Club House?'

'Yes,' replied Bert, 'Why?'

'Has she got access to the Club House Committee Room?'

'It's kept locked all the time for security purposes, but she's given the key once a week to give it a "tidy up".'

'Right then, Bert. Come over here while I speak to you in private, away from this rabble, whilst I tell you what I want you to do.'

Terry and Bert walked a short distance away from the rest of the gang, whilst Terry explained to him what he wanted his wife to do. Bert stood listening to Terry, as his head did the Nodding Donkey on an oil field well-head routine. When Terry and Bert turn back to return to the other members of the gang, they each had a hand cupped to an ear; with their heads nodding up and down, to-and-fro.'

'Taking the piss, are you?' said Bert, 'Then you lot won't be invited to be with the syndicate that's going to win next week's Lottery Club Draw.' Bert then sat down on a tea chest, among the other gang members. He had a broad smile on his weather and battle beaten face.

George then said, 'You've worked out how the Club Committee work The Lottery Clubs Draw scam. So how does Terry intend to prove it?'

'There are a few loose ends to be tidied up, before Terry can be sure of the method the Committee Members use to bring off their phenomenal number of Lottery wins. We won't know for a couple of days if Terry's hypothesis is correct. Be patient, and if he's right, next week will see all of us quite a few dozen quid richer.'

'And if he's wrong?' said Charlie.

'Then we'll all be a tanner (an old six pence) poorer,' replied Bert.

It was at this juncture the quay foreman came into the transit shed, accompanied by a lorry driver, to tell us there were a dozen lorries on the quay waiting to be loaded. So I scuttled out of the transit shed, and clambered up the three vertical steel ladders into the crane cabin, whilst the rest of my 'wage slave' workmates each grabbed a wheel barrow, and began pushing chests of tea onto loading boards, to be lifted onto each lorry platform. It was a job that was to last until 7:00 p.m., when we knocked off work, and each made our own weary way home.

When Bert arrived home that evening, Vera, his wife, was in tears. 'I've got the sack from the Club House,' she sobbed. 'The club secretary said he won't be needing my services any more, and they've given me a month's notice.'

'Good,' said Bert, 'because I was going to ask you to leave anyway.'

'Why?' Vera sobbed.

'Because Terry, my workmate, has decided our ship's gang are going to win the Club Lottery next week.'

Vera gasped, then said, 'And how does that big-headed know-all communist sympathiser intend to do that?'

'Oh! Terry's not going to arrange it, you are,' Bert replied.

'Me!' Vera said in utter surprise. How?'

'You make a cup of tea while I get washed and change out of these working clothes, then I'll explain what Terry wants you to do. OK?'

When Bert had returned to the kitchen after having completed his ablution, Vera was sitting at the table dry-eyed and composed. His dinner was on the table, and Vera was in a belligerent, retaliatory, receptive mood, as she waited impatiently for the intelligence he was about to impart to her that would allow her to get her own back on her ungrateful present employers:

'Come on then,' she said, 'don't keep me in suspense. How am I going to arrange for your workmates to win the Club Lottery?'

It was then that Bert, with his dinner in front of him, and a knife and fork in his hands, told her what Terry had told him in private in the transit shed.

'Tell Vera that when she goes into the Club Secretary's office to clean, she must open the fridge and look in the freezer compartment to see if there are any numbered stone balls inside. If there are, she must take them out of the fridge and heat them in some hot water and put them back in the lottery draw drum. Then she must exchange them with the four lottery draw drum balls, whose numbers are shown on the ticket we have brought. She must then replace the balls she has removed from the freezer, with those she has taken out of the drum, that's those with our ticket numbers on

83

them, and put them back in the same freezer compartment of the refrigerator from which she had taken the other balls.'

'Is that all I've got to do?' said Vera, 'I've been doing that job for the Club Chairman and Club Secretary for ages. They sort the stone balls out the night before the lottery draw is made, then they put them in a cardboard egg box, which they leave on the Club Secretary's desk. When I get to work on the morning of the lottery draw, my first job is to place the egg box in the freezer box of the refrigerator.'

'Christ almighty, didn't it occur to you what they were up to?'

'No!' said Vera in all innocence, 'What were they up to?'

'They were rigging the Lottery Draw, that's what they were doing, and implicating you, too. That's what they were doing,' Bert repeated.

'Were they?' said Vera. 'How could they do that?'

'Never mind,' replied Bert, 'Just do exactly as I've told you, and we'll win the Club Lottery next week. And don't worry about losing that poxy job at the Club House; I think I know how I can get you a job in the Port Authority Canteen.'

The following morning at work, during the 'mobile tea break', Terry told the delivery gang he had purchased two books of lottery tickets on the previous day. He collected sixpence each from members of the twelve-handed delivery gang, including a reluctant Bert; then he told George to see Dolly, the mobile canteen lady, and get six pence off of her too, so she could be included in the lottery draw. George went off to see Dolly, and to tell her she was included in the gang's club lottery draw, but to be included she needed to give him sixpence. Dolly told him she didn't have a sixpence, so George picked up three tea mugs off the van counter, and went off to the Port Authority's staff office, where he sneaked into the staff toilet and nicked three cups of hot water (staff toilets were off limits to common port workers; latrines were available every half-mile apart, but there was no hot water). Having filled each of the cups with hot water, he returned to the "mobile tea van" where he poured the hot water into the tea urn. He then picked up a sixpenny piece from the till, and was about to walk off, when Dolly said: 'What are you doing, George?'

'I've got your lottery ticket money for you,' he replied.

'But I'll be short when I cash in,' she said.

'No you won't, old girl,' he told her, 'I know how the system works. When you get back they'll check your takings against the grub and tea and coffee you've used up. They dip the urns to calculate how much coffee and tea you've sold. A mug of tea is two pence, three mugs is six pence. You take my word for it, you won't be short of money in the till, and we've got your six pence towards what will be the winning lottery ticket. By the way, keep 'mum' about this little escapade, and I shall bring you some Lottery Fund winnings next week.' George then, having passed on his message, made his way back into the transit shed to give Terry Dolly's sixpence contribution to "George's quay delivery gang's Lottery Fund".

The day before the Club Lottery Draw was to be made. The club committee members had met to decide which of them was due for a Lottery Win. Four numbered stone balls were taken out of the rotary drum, to match up with the appropriate numbers in one of their books of lottery tickets. That book was then handed to the committee member, whose turn it was to win that week's lottery prize. The four stone balls, that were to be the winning numbers for that week's lottery draw, were place in an egg box ready for Vera to put in the freezer compartment of the Club Secretary's office refrigerator, on the following morning—thus far, thus good—or so they thought.

On the Friday evening of the Club Lottery Draw, the Club Committee was surprised to see George and his gang turn up, to watch the Lottery Draw take place. The committee members looked at each other nervously, obviously contemplating that something unusual was amiss, as each gang member got a drink from the bar, strode to the back of the club lounge and sat down. Then, after the Club Secretary had had a few quick words with the Club Chairman, he announced he would be inviting four of the Club Committee Members in turn, to take a number independently from the lottery draw drum. He began the process of the draw by spinning the drum. When the drum had stopped turning, he invited the first committee member to take a ball from the drum. The committee member went to the drum, opened a small aperture and put his hand inside, rummage about until he felt what he was feeling for, an ice cold ball, and withdrew the number 42. He placed the ball on a stand that stood on the green baize of a card table, a set-up that was used to display the winning lottery numbers. When the first number had been drawn and displayed, the Club Committee Members, sitting together in the front row of seats, turned to look at each other and began to shuffle uncomfortably about in their chairs. Finally, after the last number was drawn and the Club Secretary announced that numbers 13, 25, 34 and 42 were the winning numbers. Terry stood up brandishing a book of lottery tickets, 'House,' he shouted mimicking a lotto winner.

'Your ticket, Terry?' The Club Secretary said, in utter surprise.

'That's right! Mine, Bert's and the rest of George's gang. Oh! And not forgetting Dolly, our beloved mobile tea lady.'

'But you and Bert don't gamble—you never ever gamble!'

'That's just a malicious rumour that's been put about, because we don't gamble when we know the odds are stacked against us. But we do like a bet when we are sure of a good win.'

'What do you mean by that, when you're sure of a good win?'

'Don't take any notice of him,' Bert butted in, 'he's talking a load of balls.'

'Balls?' said the Club Secretary, 'What do you mean by Balls?'

Terry burst out laughing, 'You know, this lottery, it's all to do with balls, cold balls. Now, how much is in the kitty this week?'

On the following Monday morning when Dolly arrived on the quay with her mobile tea van, George sauntered up to her with a bag and put it in her hand.

'What's this?' she said.

'It's your share of the lottery winnings,' George told her.

'Did we win?' she said in surprise. 'How much?'

'Fifty-five quid each, and you was right about the lottery being a fiddle. Terry worked out how the fiddle was done, that Club Committee will have to run the Club Lottery straight in future—or until they think up another way of cheating the system. By the way, Dolly. I've got a favour to ask of you.'

'Ask away, George. What is it?'

'Bert's wife Vera has been given a month's notice by Jim D., the Club Secretary. Is there any chance of you putting in a good word for her with the Port Authority Canteen Manager, when she applies for a job?'

Dolly held up the bag of winnings and said:

'I would say fifty-five pounds worth of chance, George.' Then she kissed him on the cheek and said, 'And that's for Terry.'

George put his arm round Dolly and kissed her full on the lips.

'George. What was that for?'

'Well,' George replied. 'If you think I'm going back into that shed and kiss Terry on the cheek for you, you've got to be kidding. After all, what do you think the rest of the gang will think, hum?'

A Between Deck Lecture Given
by an Amateur Physicist
Docker(An Amateur?)

We had arrived back on board a ship we had started to discharge the previous day. It was a clapped out old Greek-owned tramp steamer, of dubious origin, that had obviously escaped being sunk during the 1939-45 war, and quite possibly the 1914-1918 war too, due no doubt to U-Boat Captains thinking the cost of a torpedo was greater than the value of the target. It was a veritable *rust bucket* of a ship, if ever there was one. On this voyage she was carrying on deck an Indian elephant, and beneath deck a cargo of copra in the upper 'tween deck, loose planks of sawn teak timber in the lower 'tween deck, and logs from the Far East in her lower hold.

The copra had been shot loose in the upper 'tween deck, some two hundred tons or more of it. To discharge it, our ship's gang had to shovel the copra into large canvas nets that were then taken out of the ship by steam winches, shackled by their hoisting wires to a 'union-purchase' and tipped into a Thames lighter. For the reader's edification, copra is the dried kernel of coconuts, from which oil is extracted. Once extracted, the oil is used for a variety of purposes, with the residue being pressed into cubes, and used for cattle feed. It is also a commodity that gets infested with small mites that attack human beings by burrowing into the skin. An annoying skin condition known as *copra itch,* and for which an obnoxious ointment is issued to those men affected by it.

The Port of London, Ocean Trades, Piece-Work Rates (Discharging) Book 1954 states:

"Copra: To cover all abnormalities including the risk of 'copra itch', over-side discharge rate, four shillings and nine pence half penny per ton. That is equal to four pence half penny per-man, or transmitted into today's currency, two new pence per-man per ton."

We down-holders had dug through, and discharged, most of the copra on the previous day that had been stowed over the upper 'tween deck hatches. There was still some fifty tons left in the wings, and behind the stringer boards of the upper 'tween deck, that had to be discharged before we could strip the hatches and beams off the lower 'tween deck, to get at its other cargo of timber and logs. But rain was falling from the sky in torrents, so the ship remained 'closed up', with her deck hatches and tarpaulin hatch covers firmly held in place by the steel hatch bars and wooden wedges, while rain drops danced a fandango on the tarpaulin deck covers, to a humming sound that emulated from the ship's dingy engine-room. There would be no work done until it stopped raining, and the skies cleared. The copra couldn't be allowed to get wet, for it soon began to mildew, and became unfit for human consumption.

As each one of us, that made up the 'down-hold gang' arrived on the ship. We made our way to the 'deck booby hatch' that was our entrance into, and egress out of the upper 'tween deck, and where we all assembled ready to start work as soon as the rain stopped. The first members of our ship's gang to arrive on board the ship, had rigged up a canvas, suspended it from the under deck support stanchions and stringer-boards, over two electric light clusters (light clusters were sets of some ten or twelve 100 watt light bulbs, held in a circular frame, whose electric power supply came from the ship's own generator), that contained the heat of the light bulbs and made a cosy, warm area in which to sit in and chat, while the gang's *tea boy* went off to the ship's galley to make a pot of strong tea, while the rest of us sat in a circle, round the light clusters, under the canvas awning, talking about things in general but nothing in particular, reading or scratching ourselves in those places, where the copra mites were attacking us, more especially in our private parts, that was until one of the gang, who was reading a magazine suddenly said: 'Have any of you read about Krakatoa?'

'Krakatoa!' exclaimed one of the gang, 'What the bloody hell is Krakatoa?'

'Terry will know all about Krakatoa, he's one of those know-all bastards who reads about these sorts of things, don't you Terry?'

Terry had sat quietly, engrossed in reading *The Daily Worker* (or was it the Morning Star?) the Communist Party's own newspaper. He looked up when he heard his name, 'Not so much of the bastard,' he said. 'Now what's the question?'

'Do you know anything about Krakatoa?'

'No I don't. I've never met the woman,' he joked.

'Don't act the fool, Terry. You know I mean the island of Krakatoa.

Terry sat for a few moments before he answered, then he said: 'Is that a rhetorical question? Or do you want me to give you the accepted version as to what happened to

Krakatoa? Or would you like to hear my hypothesis as to what I think happened to Krakatoa?'

'What's a hypothesis?' asked one member of the gang, and, 'What's Krakatoa?' asked another.

'First,' said Terry, 'a hypothesis, in the simplest terms, is an individual's personal idea or theory, based on information considered relevant to those facts that may relate to a specific problem that's being studied. Krakatoa, as it now is, is what is left of a volcanic island in Western Indonesia, in the Sunda Straits, set between Java and Sumatra. In 1883 there was one of the most horrendous volcanic explosions ever known, that blew most of the island to smithereens and caused a Tsunami (tidal wave) that brought about great destruction to nearby and distant coastlines thousands of miles away. The debris from the explosion was scattered across a vast area of the Indian Ocean, and volcanic dust was spread all round the Earth. In some places, it's said, the sun was totally obscured for days. Many people thought the end of the world had come. However, I don't entirely agree with those *egg-head* intellectuals as to what actually caused the explosion.'

'Is there evidence a volcanic explosion did actually occur, Terry?' A voice asked from a dark corner of the hold, where the questioner could not be identified.

'Oh yes! There's plenty of evidence that it occurred.'

'Such as, for example?' The invisible man questioned

'There's a bloody great hole where the island used to be for one thing.'

'So what don't you agree with?'

'That it was only a volcanic eruption.'

'What makes you say that?'

'The magnitude of the explosion, it was tremendous, there's been nothing like it since on the same scale.'

'OK. Terry,' one of the dockers asked, 'what do you think caused that monumental explosion?'

'Gas,' said Terry.

'Gas?' The whole gang laughed out loud together. Then one of them blurted out, 'I thought you said the explosion was volcanic?'

'Yes,' said Terry, 'that's the accepted hypothesis, but I think that's only part of the explanation. However, what I think happened is that the eruption was triggered by volcanic lava that seeped into an under-sea, natural gas field. The lava ignited the gas and the explosive force channelled its way along the least line of resistance, which was the old volcanic chimney on Krakatoa. That, for what it's worth, is what I think happened. After all, the sea areas beneath Indonesia are known to contain vast quantities of oil and methane gas.'

'If there are oil fields in the area, Terry, couldn't it have been an oil reservoir that exploded?'

'I don't think so,' Terry replied, 'because some scientific boffin looking to get a Nobel Prize for himself, would have discovered traces of oil residue in debris left from the explosion by now. That is unless, of course, scientists have never thought of looking for traces of oil.'

'So you think all the experts were wrong and you're right, Terry?'

'You've not heard me say that,' said Terry, 'but it wouldn't be the first time. I've just explained my personal theory as to what I think caused the largest volcanic explosion on this earth in recent times. Mark you, I said explosion not eruption; that dubious honour goes to Tambora, a volcano on the island of Sumbawa, that's also in

Indonesia. I think though, that if Krakatoa explosion had been an ordinary volcanic eruption, the devastation would not have been anywhere near as catastrophic as it obviously was. I'm sure there had to have been a second power source to have caused that phenomenon, and my opinion is it was an off-shore, under-sea, natural gas field that exploded, triggered off by volcanic lava,' and Terry went back to reading The Daily Worker (or was it the Morning Star?) Totally ignoring the other gang members, as heavy rain swept across the ship's deck, beating down on the tarpaulin hatch covers, in rapid sequences, as though it was being fired from a Tommy gun.

The arguments as to what really did, or did not, happen to cause Krakatoa to explode from within, continued on for quite some time until, one of the gang suddenly changed the subject to the Universe, 'If the explosion within Krakatoa was caused, as Terry has suggested, by a seepage of molten lava into an off-shore, under-sea, natural gas field. Then what does he think caused the explosion that created the Universe?'

Terry looked up from his Morning Star (or was it the Daily Worker?) and smiled. He then said: 'No one knows how the Universe was created, but once again, there have been a great number of hypotheses and theories that have been specifically put forward by eminent Men-Of-Letters on that subject. These have varied considerably, one from the other, but it is now generally accepted by scientists, physicists, astrologers and even astronomers that the Universe came into being by what they term as a Big Bang. They also appear to have reached the conclusion, based on what they term to be scientific data, that the Universe is expanding in all directions at a uniform rate. Of course, we are back to our old friends the hypotheses and the theories, and no two hypotheses or theories on the subject are the same.

However, it's generally agreed now by all of them, that all the matter and energy of the universe was once concentrated in a solid mass of infinite density that exploded, and was subsequently thrown in all directions at great speed, within a void. Then within that void the fragments of that explosion, travelling away from their centre of gravity in various sizes, changed their shapes and forms, with a distribution of high temperature stars, galaxies, and satellites like our moon, and vast amounts of loose debris meandering its way through space and time in an apparent never ending journey to *nowhere yet everywhere.*'

'But there's no such place as nowhere Terry, is there?' one of the gang asked.

'Ah!' said Terry, 'You and I think that because we're supposed to be uneducated, untutored, ignorant dock labourers, with less intelligence than a shelled peanut. But your men-of-letters, those university educated Fellows, the compilers of hypotheses and theories, they would question that assertion. How anyone would set about constructing a hypothesis on trying to prove there was 'no such place as nowhere' is beyond the ability of my shelled peanut intellectual mental faculty. But you can be sure that somewhere out there among those university educated Fellows, Dons and cosmology scientists, someone among them is ready to prove, by well calculated and superbly verbally presented hypothetical claptrap, that there is a better than remote possibility, that *"no such place as nowhere"* does exist—*everywhere.*'

'Aren't you getting away from your discourse on the subject of the Big Bang theory, Terry?' piped up one of the gang.

'Not at all,' said Terry, 'because Albert Einstein, in my opinion, partly solved the problem.'

'How could he have done if nowhere doesn't exist?'

'Well', said Terry, 'Einstein tried to explain the consequences of the Big Bang as being like an explosion inside a balloon; as the debris from the explosion continues to expand outward, so the balloon itself expands to accommodate the mass that was spreading out in all directions within it. In other words, it expands into nowhere, which by its very existence means there must be nowhere somewhere.'

'Yes! OK! But where was the mass heading?'

'Into the void that was being pressed out by the skin of the balloon, in other words nowhere yet everywhere.'

'That doesn't make sense, Terry. What's going to happen when the balloon bursts?'

'That,' replied Terry, 'brings a new dimension into the debate.'

'What sort of new dimension?' He was asked.

'The implosion theory,' he replied. 'You see, Einstein never got round to explaining what would happen when his Big Bang balloon burst. But there was another theory put forward by an English physicist, a bloke called Hawking at Cambridge University (or was it Oxford?), Hawking has worked on advanced research into the "quantum theory of gravity". If I remember correctly, his theory was to do with "black holes" which were said to be the end products of the total gravitational collapse of a massive star into itself, following the exhaustion of its nuclear fuel. The matter inside the star, so the Hawking hypothesis goes as I understand it, is crushed to unimaginably high density. It becomes an empty region of distorted space-time that acts as the epicentre of gravitational attraction where matter is drawn towards it in ever decreasing circles, and once inside, can never escape.'

'So where does this fit in with Einstein's theory of the "expanding balloon" that stretches due to the Big Bang explosion, and Hawking's hypothesis relating to "black holes and an implosion"?'

'That should be obvious even to a dim-witted, peanut brained nincompoop, dock labourer like you,' replied Terry. 'When Einstein's balloon bursts, Hawking's "implosion" will have the whole soddin' universe collapsing in on itself, then disappearing into a "big black hole", where it will reform itself into its former self. In other words, to put it into dockers language, the whole of the bloody universe will one day disappear back up into its own proverbial rectum, and come out again through its mouth.'

There was a loud burst of laughter from the whole gang, which was cut short by a shout through the "deck booby hatch". 'Rain's stopped,' the ship worker called out, 'get those hatch covers and deck beams off, top-hand and winch drivers, take the union-purchase over-side and lift the beams of the lighter's two after bay, the lighter-man's taken the hatch covers off. Chop-chop, let's be having you, before this beaten up old wreck decides to sink under our feet, or the rain decides to come back for an en-core,' and the ship worker went on his way along the deck, to rally the other ship's gangs of dockers back to work.

With a few sighs, a lot of moaning and groaning, and even more scratching where the copra mites were biting, we got up from our warm perches, climbed up the 'tween deck ladder, through the "booby hatch" onto the ship's deck. There we began the job of stripping and folding the tarpaulins, removing the wooden hatches and steel deck beams, before we climbed back into the 'tween deck to start shovelling the last fifty tons of copra, into canvas nets ready to be discharged "over-side" into a Thames lighter, that was berthed alongside the ship.

We went back to doing what our political leaders had planned for us, under a class-based education system they had had prepared for us with its prep and public schools, grammar schools, and its demeaning basic educational boys and girls schools. And as Terry, our socialist trade unionist mentor (thought by some members of the ship's gang to be a communist agitator), constantly reminded us when he said, 'We of the *working class,* in the eyes of the ruling class, are only deemed to be fit to be "*wage slave labourers*" and work to keep them in the comfort to which they have become accustomed at our expense. Now get back to work, you lazy lot of sots, we're piece-workers or don't you know that?'

So, like a group of aged dotards suffering from a severe bout of lack of mental faculty, we went back to shovelling copra, and scratching our private parts, to Terry's chiding of, **'Baa! Baa!'**

Who Was the Greatest Luddite in Human History?

Unless you have seen an ocean going, or short sea trading, vessel being worked, you can have no idea of the skills required by the men working such vessels, or of the constant dangers they work in, or of the noisy racket that such work operations cause; noises that appear to be trying to invoked Dante's *Divina Commedia*, that is hell and purgatory combined. The noises coming from steam winches, that hiss and spit like feral cats; the cracking of union purchases as the weight of the cargo snaps them together; the whipping of derricks guys, and lazy guys, as the derricks are snapped towards the cargo being lifted; the shouts of top-hands and bull winch men, yelling out their orders. Then, above this noise, the hooting and tooting of ships, tug boats, and motor launches, that are themselves creating an invertible din above the noise of the ship's machinery: noises made by man that emulate the devil's spirits of the damned, in a hell of their own creation.

The ship being worked in this instance was a cargo passenger vessel of the "West African Coastal Trading Consortium". She was tied up (berthed) to bollards by her stem and stern to the quay. There were no springs (ropes or wires) holding her mid-ships to her berth in Tilbury Docks, because between the ship and the quay was installed what was known in the docking industry in London as a dummy, *a pontoon*, that was wedged mid-ship between the ship and the quay. It was in fact both a floating *fender* and *buffer*, installed to allow cargo carrying lighters and barges to be floated between the shore-side of a ship and the quay, whether they were discharging or loading freight.

The main imports brought into Tilbury Docks by West African coastal trading vessels during the late 1950s (the West African Coastal Trading Consortium transferred from the Pool of London to Tilbury Docks in 1956; a move that brought, for the first time in Tilbury docks' history, long term regular employment to the men of those 'down river' enclosed docks) were in the main: logs and cut timber; ground nuts; cocoa and coffee beans, palm kernels and palm oil (a commodity prepared from the Guinea oil palm, that came either in solid form packed in wooden cases, or as liquid oil that was imported in a ships deep tanks, then on discharge was pumped out into specially built small tankers when it arrived in the docks); chests of tea; and occasionally yams and bananas when they were in season.

Logs, imported from West Africa, came in various lengths, girths and weights, just as they had been cut in the jungle. Some of them still had the jackets on them (bark, that is), while others came naked (without the bark), and weighed anything between one and up to fifteen tons or more. However, the weights shown on the ship's manifest were those calculated by the timbers' known density, not by having been weighted on a scale. So it was not unusual to get a manifested weight of a log showing ten tons, when its actual weight was twelve or fourteen tons, or even more. Now I'm sure you will understand from this information that not only were the ships gangs being cheated of piecework earnings, but their very lives were put in jeopardy in so far as the wrong lifting wires, or chains, were being used in the discharge of these monstrous logs. When wires snapped, or chains broke, they often caused injury or death to those men in the process of using them.

Now in case you are unaware, I have to reiterate, dockers and stevedores were piece-workers, paid four shillings and seven and a half pence per dead weight ton, to be shared equally between a ship's gang. A ship's discharging gang comprised twelve men plus one pro-rata man when they were working under ships winches, as laid down under a 1932 Tariff agreement between The London Ship Owners' Dock Labour Committee, the Transport and General Workers' Union, and the National Amalgamated Stevedores and Dockers Union. So the actual money wage received by each member of the gang for every ton of logs discharged was four and a half pence, or two new pence per man in today's money value.

Perhaps, for the benefit of those readers who have little knowledge of conventional labour intensive dock work, or are honest enough to accept they have no knowledge at all with regard to dock work, I should explain the reason cargo ships were occasionally berthed against a dummy, was so that both shore quay cranes and a ship's own winches and derricks, could be used in the discharging or loading process. Such equipment was more generally used on operations, where cargo—passenger liners ran to a schedule; as opposed to tramp steamers, and short sea traders that put to sea, when the loading or discharging operations of the vessels were completed.

The ship I was working on this particular day, as I've previously pointed out, was a West African coastal trading

101

vessel. She had five holds, two forward and three aft, and I was working at number four hatch with my usual ship's gang, using ten ton winches and derricks. We had finished emptying the upper 'tween deck of five hundred tons of palm kernels that we stowed into Thames lighters. The down-holders had removed the 'tween deck hatches, and us winch drivers had lifted out of their couplings and removed the 'tween deck beams and sister beams, ready to break out the first log as soon as the 'bull-winch man' had raised it up and a lifting wire had been secured round it. But by anyone's standard it was a very large and heavy log, so the OST clerk was asked what weight was indicated on his log sheet: 'Nine tons,' he said.

'Nine tons my foot,' said George, our down hold foreman. 'You had better put a twelve ton wire round that,' he ordered, 'and use a fifteen ton shackle to reeve it.'

A twelve ton wire was promptly dragged across the 'tween deck and placed under the log, the bull-winch man lowered the log back into its coupling. When the log had been reeved and secured by a heavy duty fifteen ton shackle, we winch drivers lowered the union purchase, and on the top-hand's signals we began to raise the log ready to swing it out over the ship's deck to place it in a Thames lighter. The log had got no higher than ten feet in the air, when there was one hell of a crash. All the steel wires supporting my derrick had snapped, including the guy and lazy guy wires and the log, followed by the derrick, came crashing down across the open hatchway. At first, after the crash, there was complete silence except for the vibrations coming from the fallen derrick, and the grating of the broken wires as they wreathed about like a dying anaconda snake about the deck. Then

George's Ex-Regimental Sergeant Major's voice roared out: 'Is everyone all right?'

To which a chorus of voices from different parts of the 'tween deck called back, 'Yes, we're OK.' Or words to that effect.

However, in some cases there was that sort of language that irate Bishops are said to use only in a private conversation designed to bring pubescent on the faces of malfeasance clergymen.

In the docks however, the language was quite often a little more colourful; for example: 'No bloody thanks to that stupid sot, whoever it was, that calculated the weight of that sodden log, that derrick could have killed the lot of us.'

While we all stood around for a few minutes, absorbing the shock of the ship's derrick crashing down across the ship's hold, the company's Shore Captain came striding up the ship's gangway. He wasn't in the best of moods. In fact he was in a controlled rage. At first he said not one word, as he surveyed the damage. He then inspected the derrick's lifting wire, and the broken frayed guy and lazy guy wires. He then ran his eyes along the derrick. By this time the ship worker and 'ship's gearers' had turned up on the scene, and now stood behind the Shore Captain who turned to them and uttered these unforgettable words: 'Bloody Luddites,' the lot of them, that's what they are, bloody Luddites,' Then he scratched his head and stood in silence for a few seconds, deep in thought, before he began to bark out his orders.

'Right,' he bellowed to the gearers, 'lower the other derrick into its crutch, clear all the broken wires, coil them up and have them sent to the shore gear store for examination. The lifting wires on both winches are OK, so you can leave them, but the guy lines shall have to be replaced.' To the ship worker he said, 'You had better get the ship's crew to release the broken derrick from its coupling, put two twenty foot lifting wires round it, one on each end, for a quay crane to remove it onto the quay. I'll go ashore to arrange for a replacement derrick to be brought here as quickly as possible.' With those last few totally irrelevant words, after all, he was talking to professionals who not only knew the answers to the problems better than he did, but who had the know-how and skills to repair the damage, he disappeared down the ship's gangway to make his telephone call to get a new derrick and guy wires delivered to the ship. The ship worker and the gearers got on with their job of clearing the wreckage, and preparing to repair the damage. Not a word had been said about the reason for the calamity that had been caused by the over-weight log.

In the meantime Terry, our ship's gang member with a university degree, who was reputedly a communist sympathiser, had retreated to the ship's side in the 'tween deck. He was leaning nonchalantly against the stringer boards, reading the Daily Worker newspaper, apparently oblivious to the frenzied work of the ship's gearers going on about him, who were engaged in clearing up the jumbled mesh of steel guy wires that had been let fall from the derrick's head into the hold, where it was considered to be safer to wind them into coils ready to be put ashore.

George, our ship's gang down hold foreman on the other hand, was standing at the end of the log which was the cause of the calamity, reading the log and tin-tally number. (A tin-tally was a metal disc that is nailed to the end of each log, that should have identified the log number painted on the end of each log, when it was felled in the jungle, and that had been recorded on the ship's manifest when the log was loaded aboard the ship). George turned to the OST clerk responsible for checking the consignment, who had come down into the 'tween deck to clarify the stated weight of the log, that was shown on his ship's discharge papers, which were taken from the ship's manifest, and was listed as weighing nine tons.

'They don't correspond, the tin-tally and the log number,' the OST clerk told George. 'The log number on the discharging log sheet gives the weight as fourteen tons, but the tin-tally number is shown against a log that weighs nine tons.'

'So you took the tin-tally number, not the log number. Is that what you're saying?'

'Yes, I did. It's easier to find the tin-tally number, than the log number, on the discharging sheets.'

'Well don't bloody do that again, you stupid sot,' George threatened, waving his fist in front of the OST clerk's nose. 'Some of us may have been killed or injured.' He then changed the subject by calling out to the tea-boy, 'Make a pot of tea, Brains, and don't forget you've got the gearers' to cater for,' he then walked over to where Terry was reading his Daily Worker newspaper.

'What are "Bloody Luddites", Terry?' he asked.

Terry folded his newspaper, put it in his pocket, raised his hands over his head, yawned, stretched out his arms, stuck out his tongue and licked his lips, then replied: 'Luddites, George. Not bloody Luddites.'

'Then what are Luddites?'

'It's more a case of what were Luddites. Luddites was the name attributed to the anti-machinery rioters of the early 19th Century. They got that name from a Leicestershire fellow who called himself King Ludd. Ludd is reputed to have signed public letters denouncing new powered machines. His agitation led textile workers in the Midlands to destroy power looms and knitting frames, which the mill workers believed to be the cause of mass unemployment in the cotton and woollen industries.'

'Oh!' exclaimed George, 'That's what that cheeky sot meant, is it? I'll have to have a word with that Shore Captain when he comes back on board.'

In the meantime, while this conversation was going on, Brains had returned with the tea pot, and the rest of the down-holders, now armed with mugs of tea, gathered around Terry and George listening to their conversation. It was then Brains said: 'I didn't hear the beginning of your conversation, Terry. But I did hear you mention Luddites? What did you say Luddites were?'

'Destroyers of machinery, Brains.'

'That's what that Shore Captain called us.'

'Yes, so he did Brains. But we're not Luddites. Luddites deliberately destroyed machinery. As it is we haven't caused any damage to machinery, and what damage was caused is due entirely to whoever it was that miscalculated the weight of that log in a West African jungle, thousands of miles away.'

George asked Terry, 'Were there other groups of Luddites recorded in history?'

'Lots of them,' Terry replied, 'and they were not workers trying to protect their jobs, either. Most of them were in the military, but I wouldn't preclude ship owners in that category, who sent what were known as *coffin ships* to sea filled with rubbish, in the full knowledge they would never make their purported destinations and so they could collect the insurance money on the loss of the vessel and its cargo.'

'Give us a few examples,' George said.

'I don't know where to start really, or who to include. There was a Chinese Emperor who ordered the "Burning of Chinese Classics" in 213 BC, an outrageous act that possibly put Chinese social, economic, and inventive progress back hundreds, or even thousands, of years. But that wasn't the work of a Luddite in the true meaning of the word. Another catastrophe that could be put in that category was the invention by an Oxbridge scholar and inventor by the name of Charles Babbage.'

'Who was he, and what did he do?' said George.

'Charles Babbage was an English mathematician, born in Totnes, Devonshire. He was at first a student, then lecturer for a number of years at Cambridge University,' Terry explained. 'It was Babbage who compiled the first actuarial tables, and who designed a mechanical calculating machine that is now said to be the forerunner of modern computers. The machine was never built at the time of its invention because the government of the day refused to fund its construction, even though the Royal Society had recommended it should.'

'What were the government's grounds for refusing?' said Brains, to Terry's bewilderment.

'Because it was argued by some politicians in the Tory government of the time they could have built three battleships with the money it would cost to construct the Babbage Calculator. That, to my mind, was another one of the most stupid and despicable acts perpetrated by inept politicians against the advancement of scientific knowledge. But neither is that Ludditism in the true sense of the word.

However, in my opinion although they were not personally involved in the destruction of machinery, the greatest Luddites were all creators of recent modern war history. For there were the Field Marshals, Naval and Air Force commanders of the Second World War, whose major claim to fame was due to the destruction of their enemy's field equipment: tanks, guns, aircraft and ships. Those that come freely to mind in the Second World War are army commanders Field Marshals Von Rundstedt, Rommel, Zhukov and Montgomery, Air Marshalls Herman Goering and Arthur "Bomber" Harris, and Admirals Karl Donitz and Sir Dudley Pound, when they were in command of armies, air forces and naval operations in Europe, North Africa and Russia. To give you some idea what I mean, at sea in June and July 1942 a convoy of British and American merchant ships on its way to Russia, Convoy P Q 17, lost twenty five out of thirty six of its ships to German aircraft and U-Boats, when Royal Navy surface ships were ordered to abandon the convoy, and for the merchant ships to scatter and make their own way to Russia. It was a disastrous decision said to have been made by the First Sea Lord, Sir Dudley Pound. But I personally question he would have made such a disastrous decision off his own back, after having been advised by Alan Turing's cryptanalyst at Bletchley Park there were no German naval surface ships at sea. But if Sir Dudley Pound did give that fatal order, you could argue that was the result of the actions of a command Luddite.

Then there was the attack on Pearl Harbour in Hawaii by Japanese aircraft, on 7th December 1941, under the command of Admiral Yamamoto, when over three hundred Japanese aircraft, taking off from aircraft carriers, bombed and sank much of the American Pacific fleet.

However, to my mind, the greatest Luddite of them all was Winston S. Churchill, Prime Minister of Great Britain, who ordered the destruction of Tommy Flower's and Bill Tutte's Colossus and Tunny machines that were designed for deciphering the German encoding apparatus, Lorenz.

Colossus machines were electrical mechanical contraptions, designed and built at General Post Office's Dollis Park, at the request of Alan Turing, head of the code breakers at Bletchley Park, to break the code of a machine the Germans called Lorenz SZ40/42, but known as Tunny by the Allies. Tommy Flower's Colossus code breaking machine was the first "workable computer". When the Colossus machines were in use during the Second World War, Churchill said of them, "They're the geese that laid the golden eggs, and never cackled." But after the War ended, Churchill ordered the Colossus machines that had been invented and built by Tommy Flower and his team of engineers at GPO Dollis Hill, to unravel the complexities of the German Lorenz coding machines, to be destroyed.

'It is recorded in "The Register" that if Churchill hadn't ordered the destruction of Tommy Flower's Colossus machines, Tommy Flower would have received the recognition he deserved for his invention, and Britain would have led the world in computing technology. Churchill's decision must therefore rank by any standard as the most stupid single act of Ludditism in modern history, because he ordered the destruction of the forerunner machines that would dictate the future of mankind. But more especially so as Americans at the University of Pennsylvania, who had worked at Bletchley Park and knew of Colossus, and Tunny, were soon designing and building similar machines, the forerunner of which they called Electronic Numerical Integrator and Computer, ENIAC for short.'

'Where do you think the Americans got their idea for building machines similar to Colossus?' Brains asked.

'Well,' said Terry, 'there were half a dozen American cryptographers attached to Alan Turing's code breakers at Bletchley Park towards the end of the Second World War. So I expect when they got back to America and were de-briefed, they revealed what they knew of the secrets of Colossus. As you well know, the Yanks are not backward in coming forward, and they quickly realised the value of such machines.'

It was during Terry's vitriolic gambol on non-working class Luddites that the Shore Captain came down through the deck hatch and into the upper 'tween deck. He was still fuming in a controlled rage, but George wasn't going to give him a chance to verbally lambaste any of us, at least not for the damage to the ship's derrick and guy wires.

'I've been waiting for you to come back, Captain,' he began, 'I've got a bone to pick with you.'

'Have you now,' said the Captain, taken by surprise at what he no doubt thought was temerity on the part of this dock labourer, 'and what may that be?'

'The weight of this shipment of logs.'

'What about them? Are you blaming the logs for all this damage?' he said waving his right hand about him to indicate wreckage from the crashed derrick, its lifting and guy wires.

'Certainly not,' replied George, 'but I am blaming whoever it was that recorded the weights of these logs in a West African Jungle.'

'What do you mean?' the Captain said wrinkling his brow in surprise.

'Well, the log weights don't match up with the Tin-tally numbers,' said George.

'How do you know that?'

'Because I've had the OST discharging clerk down here, we've been checking the log numbers against the Tin-tally numbers. They don't match.'

'What's that got to do with the log weights?' the Shore Captain growled.

'That log we've got reeved ready to discharge, and that brought the derrick crashing down, is said to weigh nine tons on the tin-tally, but against the log number its weight is said to be fourteen tons.'

The Shore Captain looked at the log then turned to George: 'You've been discharging logs long enough to know from experience, that that log obviously weighs more than nine tons.'

'Yes,' said George, 'I do know that. That's why there's a twelve ton wire round it and its reeved through a fifteen ton shackle.'

'Oh! I see,' replied the Captain as he stood staring at the offending log, 'what do you suggest we do about it?'

'Well now,' said George. 'First, how did the dockers on the West African Coast manage to get these overweight logs aboard this ship with ten ton lifting capacity winches and derricks? Second, we're going to have to take that log ashore and weigh the damn thing. Third, how do you propose we manage to do that with ten ton lifting derricks?'

The Captain was in pensive mood. Then he said, 'Have you anything else you wish to complain about?

'Yes, our piecework earning. What are you going to do about that?'

The captain stood deep in thought for a minute. Then he said, 'All I can do is get the charge clerk to take the overall weight of the merchant's consignment, and average out the piecework rate over the time it takes to discharge the consignment. In the meantime I'll order up a floating crane from the Port Authority to take the heavier logs out of the hold. Do you know how many there are?'

'According to the OST clerk's discharging papers, taken from the ship's manifest, there are six of them, and they're all on the top stowage in the lower hold.'

'Then I'll go ashore and order up the Port Authority heavy lift floating crane. The Ajax is in the docks now, berthed at 34 Shed. If I can get her over here on the quick, we'll be able to get those heavy logs out of the hold, and into the craft, by which time the new derrick should be installed, the lifting wires and guy wires in place, and *we* should be ready to get back to work.'

George smiled then said, '*We,* Captain? I think you mean *us*,' and he waved his hand in the direction of his ship's gang.

The Shore Captain said not another word, and quickly climbed up the 'tween deck ladder, and disappeared through the deck hatch cover.

It was about half an hour later that the Port Authority heavy lift crane berthed itself against the ship's side. After a brief word or two with George, the crew installed a weighing machine on the end of the crane's hook, and brought it over the ship's hold to pick up the first log. We all got a shock when the crane took the weight, and the log was seen to register sixteen plus tons; and the other five logs in that merchant's parcel weighed much the same. George was fuming. He sent Brains to fetch the ship worker. The ship worker went to the shipping office to fetch the Shore

Captain. The Shore Captain, when he arrived on the scene, and saw the logs being weight, blurted out: 'Who gave you permission to have those logs weighed?'

'I did,' said George, 'and every one of them is tons heavier than shown on the OST clerk's log list. But don't you worry yourself Captain, I know what they've done. They've put the wrong tin-tally number on each log to confuse us on its true weight, and if it hadn't been for the fact the ship's winches weren't up to lifting the logs, the shipper would have got away with it.'

'Hum! Yes, George. You're quite right. I'll send a report to our shipping agents on the West African coast about this incident, and I'll get the tonnage clerk to record those weights on your piecework tonnage sheets. I'll see you get paid for the extra weights,' the captain said as he made his way down the ship's gangway onto the quay.

George called out after him, 'By the way, Captain, Terry has explained to us what you meant by "Bloody Luddites". If you don't come up with that extra tonnage for those over-weight logs, you may find out just what sort of *Bloody Assassins* we can be, too'

The Shore Captain looked up at the deck from the quay and smiled before saying, 'I'm sure I will George, I'm sure I will.' He then quickly disappeared between the dockside transit sheds to let us get on with the clever job only we semi-educated *dock labourers* had the skills and capability of doing. That was, of course, getting the ship's cargo discharged safely into the waiting dumb barges, ready for delivery to the merchant owners.

The Chihuahua Incident (The Theft of a Miniature Canine)

'This is worse than a damn dog's life, that's what it is.' Old Joe, our ship's gang's "top-hand," was bemoaning to us, his ship's gang; we were all huddled together on the lee side of the ship's deck, trying our hardest to keep dry and warm, as we waited on the outcome of the current crisis that had befallen us. Someone, it was being bandied about, had nicked (stolen) the live deck cargo, a pair of Chihuahua dogs, imports from Mexico.

It was a dark, late afternoon (about 5:00 p.m.), in early November. The ship's gang were trying to get some shelter under the winch deck housing, away from a howling wind, that was whistling its way through the ship's mast stays, and derrick guy wires, as flurries of rains, sleet, and snow, hammered in from the North East in that consecutive order. It was a gale that appeared to be concentrated specifically on this particular merchant vessel, berthed in Tilbury Docks. Well—that's what it seemed like to us.

'This is as bad as being adrift in the North Atlantic in an open boat,' Tom, the 'down-hold' foreman moaned.' He had had several experiences of that form of physical and mental torture in the Second World War, when the ships he'd served on as a merchant seaman during that conflict had been sunk by torpedoes; missiles fired from German U-Boats.

114

'I thought I'd seen the last of that soddin' nonsense when the War ended, I can do without being frozen to death at my age, and what for I ask you, a pair of damn dogs. I wouldn't feel so bad about it if they were real dogs, but you could hardly see the little curs, even with your spectacles on. By the way, what make of dog did the customs officer say they were when you asked him, Bert?'

Before Bert could answer, a voice from out of the darkness broke in on the conversation: 'They're called Chihuahua, and they're not merely curs, as you have so succinctly described them. They are a thoroughbred breed of Mexican of dogs that are highly prized by wealthy women, who like to cavort around city parks with the poor little animals virtually dangling on the end of a lead; and, what's more, one of you dockers have purloined them. So, none of you will leave this ship until they've been found. Don't any of you realise, those animals have to be in quarantine for six months? They could be carrying all sorts of diseases, but more especially rabies or hydrophobia, that's a severe and highly contagious virus disease caught from the bite or lick of infected animals such as dogs, cats, foxes or even bats. After an incubation period that may vary from several days to many weeks, it attacks the nervous system. The symptoms include paralysis of the breathing muscles, painful constriction of the throat muscles on swallowing or drinking, hence the alternative name of hydrophobia, which I'm sure you all know means, "a fear of water". The final stages of the disease are marked by convulsions, foaming at the mouth, madness, and a coma that always ends in certain death within a few days after its incubation period. If any of you should be bitten by an infected animal, that's what will happen to you.'

'We all know what rabies is,' said Len, one of the "down-hold" gang, a former Royal Marine Commando. 'But who do you think you are to threaten us? And what gives *you* the right to accuse any of us of taking the dogs? Now, if you would care to step ashore and say that to my face, I think I'd be well within my rights to alter either your mind, or the shape of your nose.'

'I'm a Port Health officer,' was the quick reply, 'and because of the risk to public health, I'm going to have to insist that each one of you is searched as you leave this vessel.'

'Sod off,' Old Joe told him, 'you've got no powers to search us. You'll be needing a magistrate's warrant to do that.'

'Not if I tell the Customs Officers I suspect some of you may be carrying drugs. They have the authority to search you without any formalities. But all right,' he said, 'I'll compromise. If those dogs are not found tonight, but are back in their deck-kennel tomorrow morning by eight o'clock, I'll take no further action. But I'm giving you all fair warning. I'll have magistrates' warrants in the morning to search every one of your homes—and I do mean searched—if those dogs don't materialise by eight o'clock.'

Tom, the down-hold foreman laughed. 'That's a bit of luck lads, he joked, if they're not searching our dives (homes) tonight that will give us time to clear all our loot out, before they get there to search our billets (homes) in the morning.' That statement brought a burst of rapturous laughter from all the gang.

This particular ship had been nothing but a proverbial pain in the posterior, ever since it had berthed, and we had begun to discharge her. It was carrying a cargo of Mexican handmade rugs, carpets, ponchos, hats, bales of this, cases of that, plus a consignment of sacks of coffee. The ship's manifest must have been two meters long, comprised as it was of bits, pieces, and small parcels of under hatches freight and, two dogs specified as being "live deck cargo". Although both miniature canines had mysteriously vanished, so we had been informed, since the ship had berthed.

In the upper-tween deck cold cupboards, there was a freight of melons that could not be discharged till the 'tween deck's cargo had been put ashore. Then, when the 'tween deck was cleared, and the merchant owners of the melons lorry transport had been assembled on the quay, to transport the fruit direct to Spitalfields market. The cold room cupboard doors were opened, to reveal pinpoints of light shining out of the darkness from within. There were also some mournful groaning sounds, and a stench that filled the nostrils, almost bursting one's lungs. It was a stench that permeated into everything it came into contact with, as I found out when I arrived home that evening to be greeted with. "What on earth is that horrible smell?" To which I replied, 'Mexican melon trash—or to be more precise, trash-of—melon.'

'What the hell is it?' said Tom, the down-hold foreman and, 'Christ, where's that bloody awful stench coming from?' and, 'Is there a light somewhere?'

A cluster of lights were brought down from the deck and switched on to reveal four men, obviously Mexicans, laying in their own excrement and vomit near the cupboard doorway.

'Stowaways,' Tom our down-hold foreman calmly called up to Old Joe, the top-hand. 'You'd better get word to the shipping office, to inform the Port Authority Police and the Immigration Service.'

It did not take a Port Authority police superintendent, a sergeant, and several police officers long to arrive on the scene. The sergeant quickly sized up the situation, (no doubt due to the stench coming up out of the hold), to call down the hold with this order issued to the dockers: 'Bring them up on deck.'

The ship's gang were as equally quick to reply with: 'Not so bloody likely, if you want 'em, then you can come down here and get 'em.'

'Can any of them speak English?'

'How should we know?' was the reply. 'You come down here and ask 'em.'

The police superintendent, obviously no less as brave as his colleagues, decided to do a bit of interrogation from the relative safety of the ship's deck.

'Any—you—speak–de–English?' to which he received his replies in moans and groans.

'Don't start that nonsense,' said Old Joe the top-hand. 'Send for an ambulance.'

'Good idea,' said a constable, 'if that's all right with you, Sir. I'll go over to the PLA foreman's office, ask him to send for an ambulance, and to inform the Immigration people we have arrested four suspected illegal immigrants.'

'Not till you have formally arrested them under the "Judges Rules" you won't,' Old Joe said. Then 'Right now, one of you can go on down there and do it, so the lads can get that mess cleared up, and get on with their work.'

A constable (obviously suffering from nasal congestion), volunteered to come down into the deck to formally make the arrests; then a cargo board was lowered into the hold. The stowaways, who were hardly able to stand, were ordered (with pointed finger sign language) to get onto the board, which was then hoisted up onto the ship's deck where a deck hose was played on them to wash off the excrement and vomit. The ambulance crew who had turned up, wrapped the stowaways in clean red blankets, and put them in the back of the ambulance. A police constable got in the back of the ambulance with them, and the ambulance was driven off to wherever stowaways are taken when they are arrested; that's the last any of us saw or heard of them. Then the arguments began with Tom our "down-hold" foreman calling out: 'Where's the ship worker?'

'I'm here on deck,' came the quick reply.

'We're not cleaning this bloody mess up,' he was told, 'and we're not starting work until it is. Get on to the ship's mate and tell him to get the crew down here to clean the place up.'

'I'm the ship worker, not your messenger boy. One of you go up and tell the mate what you want, that's if you can find him sober; then you may be able to get him to help you.'

'I'll go,' I said, and made my way to the first mate's cabin.

I knocked on the cabin door, but I got no reply; I kicked the door, but there was still no reply, I pushed the door open and peered into the cabin. The mate was sprawled on his bunk face down, obviously as *drunk as a skunk in his bunk*. There was an empty bottle on his cabin desk, and a wine glass on the cabin floor beside the bunk. I closed the door and made my way to the crew's quarters, where I heard voices coming from one of the cabins. I pushed the cabin door open, there were four crew members inside sitting at a table playing cards, each had a glass of wine in his hand, and there were several empty bottles on the table together with a pile of Mexican pesos.

'Do-any-of-you-speak-de-English?' I asked, mimicking the PLA police officer.

'A lit-tle,' one of the men replied.

'Where-is-de-boson?'

'I'm zee boson,' he replied.

'Right, number–two–de–'tween deck-hold. De–sacks–of–de–saw-dust. You—savvy?'

'Saw-dust?' he looked at me quizzically.

I made the movements of sawing a piece of wood, then ran my hand along the cabin floor to pick up some dust.

'Ah, saw-dust!' he said.

'Number two hold, pronto,' I told him and put two fingers up, 'Two' I repeated.

'Two,' he said raising two fingers.

'Yes, come,' I said, waving my index finger, 'I'll show you,'

I led him out of the crew's quarters, along the deck, and down into number two hatch's 'tween deck. I showed him the mess inside the "cool chamber" doorway. He put his thumb up to show me he had got the message, and I followed him to the forecastle deck store room, where there were a number of sacks of sawdust. We each picked up two sacks, one in each hand, and carried them to number two hatch, where we threw them down the hold into the 'tween deck. The bosun went off to get some of the crew, and bins to put the offending 'muck' into; in the meantime the ship's gang opened the sacks and poured the contents over the stinking mess, which was slowly absorbed into the sawdust. Three crewmen (the rest of the boson's card school) came down into the 'tween deck. They quickly shovelled up the sawdust, with what had been the contents of the stowaway's stomachs, and rectums, from inside the cool chamber cupboard. But the stench lingered on like a slowly dispersing invisible November mist. It was an experience one cannot, could not, ever forget.

If it wasn't one thing on that damn ship that went wrong, it was another. The Chihuahua incident being just one of them, what's more the ship had become infested with customs officers searching for drugs (due without doubt to information passed to them by the Port Health officer). They virtually turned the ship upside down and inside out. If they found any drugs, we were never privy to that information, but if they didn't find any, it wasn't for their want of searching.

The word had been put round the ship that if the two Chihuahua dogs were back in their deck-kennel by eight o'clock the next morning, the incident would be closed. If the dogs were not back in their deck-kennels, then all those people working on the ship would have their houses searched—there was to be no exception. So, as miraculously as the dogs had disappeared they reappeared, and no further action was taken.

That shipboard incident has long been forgotten, with the exception of me because the ship's gangs had known it was our crane-driver Harry, who had taken the dogs. Harry had only recently been made a widower, left with two young children to fend for. The dogs were to have been a present for his children, although they never got to see them. They had only recently lost their mother, and two weeks after the Chihuahua incident on the Mexican ship, their father was killed whilst loading an Ocean-Sea Trading merchant vessel. The crane he was driving toppled over into the ship's hold, and he was crushed to death when he was shot out of his crane cabin window into the vessels lower hold, and parts of the crane cabin fell on top of him. Luckily he was killed instantly. So that, you can say, was the end of the tale of the Chihuahuas, and of Harry the crane-driver who had purloined them. That is except to record there was more fuss caused over the disappearance of the two Chihuahua dogs, than there was of the death of Harry the crane driver, where at the inquest the verdict was stated to be a simple case of, *death by misadventure*.

You Damn Incompetent Fool!
(A Doctor's Wrong Diagnosis)

There had been no ships entering or leaving Tilbury docks for two or three weeks, or perhaps even longer, one tends to lose track of time as days drag by into weeks. All the men that worked together in gangs on a regular basis were in the dock labour compound either waiting to be sent home with an attendance stamp until the next "call on" period at 12:45 p.m. or to be sent out of sector on allocation to one of the upriver docks within the Port of London. These could be The Royal Albert, King George V, Victoria, or down the river to one of the deep-water anchorages in the lower Thames to load high explosives, for or even perhaps to some stevedore contractor discharging timber, or pulp, afloat on the river Medway.

Oh! I must tell you the oddest job that any docker I ever knew once had. It was when one of our Tilbury men was allocated to a discharging ship working on the river Medway. It was a Greek ship carrying pulp (or was it timber?) that also had a herd of goats in the upper 'tween deck. His job had been to stop any of the goats from jumping down into the lower hold. He often used to boast he was the only docker ever to have been a "goat herder" aboard a ship. Personally I don't think that was much of a job to boast about—rather a demeaning occupation for a docker, I think. Well! Don't you?

The deep-water anchorages in the lower Thames was where stevedores (blue union men) based at Northfleet Dock Labour Board Compound were sent to work on loading high explosives: dynamite, bombs, shells, small-arms ammunition—that sort of thing. They were anchorages where it was assumed, if a ship blew up during the loading process, it wouldn't cause too much of a problem. On the other hand they may have been sent afloat to work on ships lashed to Greenhithe buoys, to work on discharging imported wet or dry wood pulp, imports from one of the Scandinavian countries, or Russia, on discharging esparto grass from Spain or North Africa, or even to be sent out of sector to another port.

It was just after 8:00 a.m. when the tannoy system began booming out orders; orders that were being given from within the Dock Labour Board Office. 'All books in' it demanded, most of the men in the compound filed up to the Dock Labour Board office windows, to hand their attendance books to office clerks, who were waiting to allocate them to various jobs that required manning. On the other hand a number of men chose to forgo their "fall back guarantee" and walked out of the compound. These were mainly taxi drivers, boarding house keepers, and corner shop retailers, who made the docks a useful tool in paying their National Insurance Stamps, and keeping their Income Tax liabilities in order, while they followed their true vocations without hindrance from the governing authority. No doubt some of them would be back for the 12:45 p.m. muster, hoping they would not be sent to work, and asking the Dock Labour Board Manager for an excuse stamp to cover that morning's "call on", or with a doctors certificate to cover their non-attendances. These men were adroit at manipulating all the rules set down for the control of dockworkers employment, to their own benefit.

Most dockworkers knew what was going on between those men, and those in authority, who were colloquially known as the "powers that be". But as the scallywags had (reputedly) received their Dock Workers Registrations through being members of a secret society, or some religious fraternity, there was absolutely nothing anyone in the lower echelons of the pecking order could do about it. Except perhaps complain to the Trade Union Official, who by sheer coincidence himself happened to be a member of one or more of those same secret societies or religious orders.

However, this arrangement seems to have suited Dock Labour Board Managers to a certain extent. For it saved money having to be paid out on the "fall back guarantee". That was, of course, unless the miscreants asked for an "excuse stamp". Then that would only cause them to lose one eleventh (or if they were registered as category "C" men, one sixth) of the weekly "fall back pay", or they brought in a doctor's certificate on the following morning, covering them for the whole of the previous day. Such shysters always got their own way, and through their antics they often brought the port transport industry into disrepute. On the other hand men with genuine reasons for non-attendance, more often than not, found their reasons for absence were unacceptable by Dock Labour Board managers. They therefore lost the whole of their "fall back guarantee" payments for a week. That is how corrupt the system was allowed; in fact was too often encouraged to become. In many cases too, local GPs were as callous as Dock Labour

Board Managers, as I know from personal experience after I was seriously injured in a dock accident, which the following tale shows.

On the day of this particular tale, one of those men who handed his attendance book in at the Dock Labour Board Compound Office window also handed in with it a doctor's certificate. As he stood by the office window, he looked like death itself. He kept coughing then gasping for breath. His sunken blue eyes, set in a deeply drawn haggard face, was a face that was as mottled grey as the sides of those British warships he had served in during the Second World War. His shoulders were slouched forward over his body, giving him the appearance of his being a descendant of the Hunchback of Notre Dame. His coughing into a piece of rag, that stood in for a handkerchief, was a testament to his diminishing lifespan, as he gasped for air like a dying fish in polluted dock water. This itself should have been proof enough to any nitwit, or village idiot, in any hamlet or town throughout the new Queen's Realm that the man was on his last knockings and not much longer for this world. He hardly had the strength to stand up, let alone to be sent back to work in the docks.

One of the office clerks took his attendance book with the sealed envelope that contained a doctor's certificate. The clerk opened the envelope, that was addressed to The Dock Manager, gave a quizzical look at the docker (who was a grain porter), and told him to wait outside the Welfare Office. He then took the certificate to the Dock Labour Board's welfare officer, Dan Foley.

Dan looked at the certificate and frowned. He then got up from his chair, went to his office door and called to the man,

'I've got your doctor's certificate here, Charlie', he said as the man approached him.

'Go home, I'm going to have a word with your quack.'

'But Dan,' Charlie protested between bouts of coughing and loud gasps for breath, 'he's told me I'm fit for work. The DSS will stop my sick money.'

'No they won't, Charlie,' said Dan. 'Go home. I'll sort this lot out for you. Don't say another word.' Dan then put his head outside his office door and called out, 'Is anyone going into Grays?'

One of the dockers walked across the compound. Dan said, 'Take Charlie home, Bill. See he gets indoors before you leave him.'

There was no argument. 'Right, Dan,' Bill replied, 'I'll see to that. 'Come on, Charlie,' Bill ordered, and with those last few words they were gone, with Charlie coughing and spluttering as he slouched his way, for the last time as it happened, out of the Dock Labour Board Compound, coughing and whooping as his lungs did their best to sustain some momentum in his legs, and life in his frail, dying body. We knew we would never see him again.

When Charlie and Bill had left his office, Dan passed me the doctor's certificate as he picked up his telephone and dialled a number, 'Read that,' he said.

I did. It read as far as I could make out from the scrawl,

'There is nothing physically wrong with this man. My professional opinion is, he is fit to return to work as from (that day's date) Signed Dr. D' or words to that effect.

'Christ, Dan,' I said, 'any fool can see the man's seriously ill.'

Dan nodded just as the recipient of his call answered the telephone. Then Dan said, 'Don't you tell me not to interrupt

127

you while you're taking surgery. This is Dan Foley, the London Dock Labour Board's Welfare Officer, so don't you damn well "who". You know full well who I am. I've just been passed the certificate you gave Charlie K. to return to work. I'm not interested in what you call your professional opinion. It's as biased as you are stupid. Don't answer me back. No, I'll tell you what's wrong with him. He's damn well dying, that's what's wrong with him. Don't you think you should have sent him to be seen by a consultant dealing with bronchi and lung infections, before you began to malign him? No! If you had been practising medicine in the West India, Millwall or Royal Docks areas, you would have known that the man is suffering from "farmers lung". No! I'm aware it's not my place to tell you your job, but I've been dealing with similar medical problems like this for years. For your information the man's a "corn porter", farmer's lung is an occupational hazard in his job. No it isn't. It's a condition caused by the inhalation of spores from fungi that's got from breathing in the dust from wheat and other rough grained cereals. No! I've just told you. He's not an ordinary docker, he's a corn porter. No! You can measure his life span in weeks, not years. No! Just give him a certificate for a month; he'll probably be dead before he needs another one. Right! You do that.'

Dan slammed the telephone down. He was seething with rage. He told me: 'That stupid old fool, it's time he retired. I ought to complain to the British Medical Council about his lack of medical ethics. He should have sent Charlie to be seen by doctors at the Chest Clinic Department in St Thomas Hospital. That's where corn porters were sent for lung treatment when grain ships were worked in the West India, Millwall and Royal Group of Docks, before the ships were transferred down river to Tilbury riverside grain terminal. Though I have to admit it, none of the grain porters last long once farmer's lung has been diagnosed. The disease is a killer, it's as deadly as asbestosis.' Then he said. 'It's not generally known but corn porters' average expectation of life is just about fifty three years.'

'How old is Charlie?' I asked.

'He's fifty eight, but don't forget, he was in the navy for four years during the War.'

I left Dan in his office seething with anger, although he always tried his hardest to suppress his feelings. He had a genuine respect for the dockers, stevedores, and lighter-men and OST clerks under his jurisdiction, and he worked tirelessly on their behalf. Dan was awarded a well-earned MBE for his work on behalf of Registered Dock Workers. However as it so happened, Dan had no need to report Dr D. to the General Medical Council, as the doctor died three weeks after his verbal confrontation with Dan over the telephone. That, incidentally, was just a few days after Charlie K.'s. body had been certify as dead, by none other than Dr D. himself. It may have been the shock of Charlie K.'s death, so soon after Dan's verbal castigation of Dr D.'s diagnosis as to Charlie K.'s medical condition that aided in the demise of Dr D.—who knows—it may have been a contributory factor in his death?

There was an obituary in the local newspaper, stating what a marvellous man that Dr D. had been, and the wonderful contribution he had made to the community he had served for over thirty years, as no doubt he had.

On the other hand the only mention Charlie K. received was in the local newspapers "In Memoriam" column that read: 'I wish to thank Charlie's former comrades in the

Royal Navy, with whom he served during the last war, all our friends and neighbours who sent flowers, to those who attended my late husband's funeral, and for the generous money collection I received from his workmates in the docks. I wish to offer my special thanks to Mr Dan Foley, the Docks Welfare Officer, for all the arrangements he made on behalf of Charlie, my children, and me.'

So that, you may think, is the end of another tale. Unfortunately in my experience it's the end of a chapter in a never-ending tale relating to the same subject matter.

A London Dockland's Character: ("Sparko", An Aged Dockland's character)

You can be sure the Docklands in each and every port, of every country throughout the world, produced many types of characters: Some of them were fools, or at least acted the fool, to give the impression they were fools; some were thugs, at least they were all the time they thought they could get away with it; some were gangsters, more especially among those men who worked in city dockland areas; almost all of them were ex-service men, in many instances men who had escaped death in wars that went back as far as the Boer War of 1899-1901. However, sprinkled among them were highly intelligent, uneducated men, with a sprinkling of men who held university degrees, and large numbers who held trade qualifications made up these unique workforces within the British Isles.

Then there were the entrepreneurial elements too: taxi cab drivers; publicans and guest-house keepers; bookmakers and bookmakers runners. There were too, a few "Family Planning/Birth Control officers" (dock workers who sold contraceptives to clients, and any passing trade they could pick up, mostly in the guise of merchant seamen coming ashore after a long voyage). One particular vendor of contraceptives (known among dock workers as Mr Durex for

131

obvious reasons) was to my personal knowledge Roman Catholic by religion, but he boasted he only sold his family control products to members of Protestant and nonconformist religious organisations, and as I have previously explained. These groups of men used their dock registrations as a means of paying income tax and National Insurance Contribution through the National Dock Labour Board, thereby avoiding paying taxes on their lucrative earnings elsewhere.

Also hidden away behind the high brick walls, or wooden latticework fences, within the dock precincts, there was amongst that nondescript workforce, large numbers of Christians of many denominations and faiths, that worked in the docklands beside their atheists worker counterparts. For example, Church of England, Roman Catholic, Presbyterian and even a sprinkling of members of "The Church of Latter-day Saints." I have to mention here also that other group: the provocateurs, men in the pay of the police; police narks, men who had been recruited to inform on their workmates, after themselves having been caught petty pilfering; political radicals, that were set to stir up trouble on the orders of their controllers, with the aid of undercover media reporters who, in some cases visited the cafés and public houses outside the docks to listen in on any tittle-tattle that would help them to stir up trouble for the benefit of increasing their media organisations circulation.

Obviously there were also men who suffered the indignity of having to carry what I considered to be offensive nicknames; these came about for a variety of reasons. For example, there was "No Neck, son of One Arm". No Neck was a clerk who the dockers often joked had been a parachutist during the Second World War, who had landed on his head during parachute training. The impact of the fall having shoved his head down into his body; his father, "No Arm", had had his left arm shot off during the First World War. Then there was "Black Mac", son of Canadian Jim. Black Mac was a black character, the son of a former Canadian soldier who had married an English girl, and stayed in England after the Second World War. The "Orsett Lizard", an old man possibly in his seventies, who was very tall and thin, but had short arms and long legs. The "Galley Rat", another old man who always made for the ship's galley when he went aboard a vessel, from where he could scrounge a sandwich for his breakfast. "Electric Legs", a ship worker who walked about speedily like a clockwork soldier, when he was on the move. "Rent a Mouth", a ship worker whose voice could be heard across the width of the docks, when he was issuing out orders. "The Sheriff", a ship worker who, when he came on a ship's gang that had run into a snag while loading or discharging cargo would say, 'What's the hold up?' Then there were the ships loading superintendents such as "Peter Splendid" who, when a ship's gang had finished a job, he would congratulate them with, 'Splendid chaps, Splendid.'

Young men entering the port transport industry, who come from docking families, soon found themselves being called after their grandfather's, father's or brother's names, but with the prefix "young" added. For example, in my case, when I worked for the Port of London Authority I was known as "young Ted" after my grandfather, or "young Gus" after my brother; but when I worked for a stevedore contractor my name became "young Percy" after my father.

As you will have read above, I have already incorporated in this tale a number of devious characters that sought "sanctuary" from the tax man, through the good offices of that Government inspired Employment Agency officially known as The National Dock Labour Board. A bureaucracy set up under the Dock Workers (Regulation of Employment) Act 1947 that encouraged such employment abuses, while acting as the employment agent for the benefit of the Port Authority and the shipping industry.

However, now I will begin my tale about one of the great dockland characters, an East End Londoner known as "Old Sparko". Now it was said of Old Sparko, that he was a somewhat devious character, but that was only because he acted as though he was a buffoon, yet in reality he was an intelligent, shrewd, conniving, lovable old sot, whose apparently stupid antics earned him a second moniker, "The Raving Nutter". But believe you me, Old Sparko was far removed from any form of mental derangement, and as sure as the speed of a hand may deceive an eye, so too can a jester make himself out to be an harlequin, if you can understand the subtle difference in my meaning.

So there was I, standing on my lonesome in the Dock Labour Board Compound, waiting for the electronic tannoy system to give the inevitable order of: 'All Attendance Books in.' I was in fact mentally preparing myself for a trip to Greenhithe, on the north Kent shore, to be sent to work aboard a ship off shore in the river, discharging pulp for delivery to a local paper mill, or to catch a slow steam train for a journey to any one of the many upper docks of the port of London, or an even slower tug boat journey from Tilbury ferry passenger jetty, down the Thames to the "lower deeps", to work on a vessel loading explosives (ammunition, rockets, cordite or dynamite—that sort of thing). I had a long wait, for it was about half an hour after all the attendance books had gone in through the office windows, and I had dozed off leaning against the "pick-up point" rails, that I was brought back to reality with the order through the tannoy: '3/34345 Bradford H. T. to the Royal Albert Docks. Come and get your rail warrant and attendance book.' So that was that. I was on my way to London, the only man to be allocated to work on that morning.

I made my way to Tilbury town railway station, from where I caught a slow steam train to Plaistow station via Barking, but to be fair even the fast steam trains were slow, clapped out pre-war contraptions (First World War that is) that hissed, huffed, and puffed their way from Southend to Fenchurch Street railway station in the City of London, until they were replaced by new electric overhead cable fed trains in the 1960s, and thence on to the Royal Albert Docks by bus. My destination was a Blue Star Liner, loading for Australia, that sailed under the name of the *SS Brisbane Star*.

When I arrived aboard the vessel, a ship worker (Mr Monday) was looking first at his pocket watch, then at me. 'Hallo, sonny,' he growled, 'are you the bloke that's been sent up from Tilbury?'

'Yes,' was my short reply.

'Took yer time getting 'ere, didn't yer?' He said.

Of course, one always had to make some sort of excuse to placate a ship worker, especially one who was looking at his watch, so I said, 'Have you tried catching a steam puffer train on the Southend to Fenchurch Street railway line lately?'

He shrugged his shoulders and said, 'Go to Number four cargo hatch, the gang are waiting for you, so they can make a start loading 500 tons of cement.'

As the ship's gangway was placed opposite Number two cargo hold, I strolled along the deck to Number four cargo hatch, to be greeted by the ship's gang's "top-hand" with, 'Are you the geezer from Tilbury, sonny?'

'Yes, I am,' I said, accepting the fact he was using a contradiction of terms.

'Has the ship worker told you about the cement?'

'Yes, he said you'd got 500 tons to load.'

'He's tried to put the frighteners into yer, sonny. We finished loading the last 150 tons of cement at "Beer Ho" this morning. We're now waiting on a barge of steel girders to be towed in from the river. It's in the locks now, but the rest of the gang have gone off to get some grub. I've been waited here for you to turn up. By the way my name is Joe. I'm off to the Port Authority canteen. Are you coming?'

'Yes,' I replied, and I followed him off the ship, from where we made our way to the Port of London Authority's industrial canteen.

As we entered through the canteen's front door, in a small space against the wall opposite, an old man possibly in his late sixties or early seventies was playing a tune on an antiquated flute. He was dancing about like a wild dervish. He had a battered hat at his feet that was slowly filling up with all sorts of coins—coins of the realm, coins of numerous republics, and a few steel washers of various sizes.

'Holy Jesus,' I said. 'Who in hell's that?'

'That's Old Sparko, he's a raving nut-case,' said Joe my new-found mentor.

'Some nut-case,' I replied, 'he must have a couple of quid or more in that hat, not counting the steel washers (a docker's day-work wage at that time was one pound, nine shillings and six pence). How often does he come in here doing his music and dance routine?'

'Oh,' replied Joe, 'at least a couple of days each week. He's on a "B" Book ("B" Books were issued to men over 65 years of age who had restricted "fall-back" money equal to $4/11^{th}$ of a full week's "fall-back pay", no matter how many times they attended the "labour call on" in any one week), so the old sot comes in here where he knows the lads will cough up a few coppers.'

'Yes, but he must be fit to keep that up,' I said as I tossed a few pennies into the hat.

By this time Joe and I were in the food queue, aluminium trays in our hands, and being served with dinner, sweet and tea that cost us two shillings and six pence each. Nothing more in the verbal stakes passed between us until we sat down. Then Joe said: 'Old Sparko was brought before a Stipendiary Magistrate a couple of weeks ago.'

'What for?' I asked him.

'Causing grievous bodily harm.'

'You've got to be kidding me, Joe. That geriatric old sot? What did he do, beat up an egg?'

'No, he beat up four Teddy Boys at the bus stop outside the dock gates.'

I laughed, 'What did he do, hit them over the head with their drain-pipe trousers?'

'No,' said Joe, 'according to a Port of London copper. Sparko started to do one of his dance routines at the bus stop. The Teddy Boys, who were at the bus stop, started making fun of him. Then when a bus turned up, they tried to jump the queue. So, Old Sparko set about the lot of 'em. Don't underrate him. He's as hard as nails, and twice as nasty when he's provoked. But I suppose that comes from his army training.'

'What did he use to do that much damage to those louts with?' I said.

'His dockers hook and some unarmed combat,' said Joe. 'He put his dockers hook through one of 'em's jaw, broke another one of 'em's arm by crashing his hook against it, and he stove in another one of 'em's teeth with a head butt. If a Port Authority copper hadn't been on hand, he'd have probably killed the lot of them.'

'So why isn't he in nick (prison) on remand?'

'Well, the PLA copper in evidence explained to the Stipendiary Magistrate what had happened. He'd been watching the antics of the Teddy Boys through the Police-Box window. So the Stipendiary let Old Sparko out on bail, but for reasons best known to himself, the Stipendiary made a Court Order that Old Sparko had to go for a psychiatric assessment.'

'Why? I said. 'It's obviously a case of self-defence, after all what did they expect the old man to do, let the thugs beat him to a pulp? Has he been to see the shrink yet?' I asked Joe.

'Yes,' he replied, 'and you will never believe what happened when Old Sparko met a psychoanalyst.'

'What did happen?'

'The psychoanalyst had apparently started to question Old Sparko about his athletic prowess. The Stipendiary Magistrate wanted to know whether Old Sparko had gone "berserk" you know, "flipped his lid; gone off of his rocker; lost control of his actions" before he'd attacked the Teddy Boys.' He asked all sorts of pertinent questions about what sports Old Sparko had played, and if he's won any prizes or medals. Old Sparko told us he was bemused by the stupidity of the questions.'

'Why should he have been?' I asked Joe.

'Because it's well known in the docklands the old man was an athlete during his young days. In the army he was also a Physical Training Instructor (PTI), a Regimental boxing champion, a renowned cross country runner, a rugby player, a weight lifter—you name it in the sporting game and Old Sparko's done it. He's got a case full of cups, medals and ribbons. Anyway, it clued up the shrink who asked Old Sparko if he could run round the hospital gardens, jump over a few hedges, that sort of thing, just to give him some idea about Old Sparko's physical fitness. The old man thought the shrink was taking trying to extract the proverbial urine. So before the shrink could stop him, Old Sparko had stripped off his coat, pullover and shirt down to his vest, removed his trousers down to his pants, opened the door of the shrink's consulting room, and was off like a greyhound, running round the hospital's gardens, clearing hedges as good as any steeple-chaser less than half his age.'

'Jesus Christ,' I said, 'has he been back to Court yet for sentence? What did the shrink's report have to say?'

'I don't know,' Joe replied, 'there's been no word about it round the docklands yet. So I don't suppose he's been back to court.' Then he said, 'If he has been sentenced at least they've not locked him up—look at him over there—hopping about like a kangaroo on hot sand. How many blokes do you know who could keep up those shenanigans for as long as he's been doing it, just to earn a few extra shillings?'

Joe and I sat chatting until it was time to return to the ship. As we went towards the canteen door, Old Sparko was still there playing his flute, well sort of, and dancing about; mimicking the antics of a cat running over hot bricks. I took a half crown out of my pocket, dropped it into his battered hat, bent over towards him and said: 'Get yourself a full dinner, Sparko. Keep your strength up. You may bump into a few more Teddy Boys on your way home.'

The old man just smiled, nodded his head and winked. That wink was as good as telling me this was the East End of London. He knew how to look after himself. In other words, as Charles Darwin would have put it, it was a place only for the survival of the fittest. There were gangs of thugs and violent criminals in and around London's Docklands. In those days the Richardsons and the Kray Brothers and their gang ruled the proverbial roost outside the docks, but not inside the docks where there were more "state trained military assassins" than one would care to count. Of course Old Sparko new the rules of his environment, both in the docks and outside, far better than any Stipendiary Magistrate ever could. Physical violence was a way of life, and quite often a way of disfigurement or even death to the unwary.

As I'd expected, the gang I worked with on that day were stevedores, so at 7 o'clock that evening. I was paid off and told to return to my own Dock Labour Compound the following day. It was good, however, to be back in a dockland setting where one was most unlikely to be waylaid by a gang of thugs outside the docks. But of course that didn't mean there wasn't the occasional skirmish or two inside the Port of London's Tilbury Docks perimeter boundary, because there were.

Oh! I almost forgot to tell you what happened to Old Sparko when he returned to the Stipendiary Magistrates Court. Well he was given a six months suspended prison sentence because, when the psychoanalysts report was read out in court, it divulged Old Sparko had been a Sergeant Commando Training Instructor in Unarmed Combat during his wartime army service, which simply means that under the law he was seen to be taking advantage of his "combat skills" in defending himself. The fact the old man was simply defending himself against a physical attack on his person by four thugs didn't appear to be taken into consideration. But it's a pity the four Teddy boys hadn't known he'd been an unarmed combat instructor before they attacked him, because then they may have shown the old man a bit of respect. Well, I bet they will if they ever meet him again. Don't you?

The Antics of Alfie (A Second World War "Combat Stressed" OST Clerk)

There was no doubting at all the man was, as the army veterans always referred to their "combat stressed" workmates, "bomb-happy". "Bomb happy" being a term used by ex-military personnel, to describe mentally ill former comrades. That is men suffering from battle fatigue due to enemy action; or in Alfie's case, more probably due to his having spent a fair part of his war service in military prisons.

This former conscripted soldier, now registered as an OST clerk, let none of us fellow dockworkers that had come to know him in the docklands after the Second World War have the slightest idea in which theatre of war he had served, that's if he had served in any battle zones at all. It was the general consensus of opinion among the men, that Alfie had spent most of his war service "locked up". Although as in the case of most men who had served as front line troops, Alfie rarely, if ever, mentioned the war at all. So it's quite possible we did misjudge him.

However, the one thing we really did know about Alfie was that he had served as an Irish Guardsman, that he regularly frequented his local Catholic church in the East End of London, through which source I surmised he had no doubt made the contacts through which he obtained his Dock Worker's Registration. He had then entered the port transport industry after his demobilisation from the army in 1946; he was mentally unbalanced due, most dockers and Registered Clerks thought, to his military service, but to all intents and purposes he was otherwise considered to be harmless. As some of us were to find out in the course of time, it was a mental illness he used as an attribute to his fullest personal advantage—in other words—he was, in dock terminology, a "liberty taking nutter".

Although Alfie was a Londoner, born and bred in Stepney, he always boasted he was really Irish, descended from Irish Catholic families that had been force to leave their native Ireland during the infamous potato famine of 1846-47. They had come to England, and settled with thousands of their fellow countrymen, among the slum dwellings on the north bank of the river Thames, to eke out a precarious living from the docklands, first by being employed to help in digging out the marshland into which the enclosed docks were constructed, then when the docks had been built, working as stevedores for several generations, until Alfie broke the "stevedore mould" and became an OST clerk.

Alfie was, had it not been for his assumed diminished mental capability, a nondescript character. He was just one of the hundreds of other nondescript ex-military service personnel that made up the working population of the Docklands of The Port of London. He was just about six feet tall, slim, with grey-blue eyes, and thinning light brown hair, that was going grey round his temples. He also had one other curious failing that was discovered by a former army Regimental Sergeant Major (RSM), who had noted that when anyone barked out the order 'shun', Alfie sprung to

143

attention and stood like a ramrod for a few seconds that was up until the spell order was broken, by some miraculous internal repair to a brain fuse that then freed him from his momentary mental imprisonment. But as he had been a guardsman, 'shun' was possibly an order that was second nature to him.

Another of Alfie's military quirks, that had followed him from his army days was that when he was tallying ship's cargo on the quay, he would sometimes act as if he was on guard at some military installation. He would march one hundred paces up the quay, do a quick about turn, and march back again to his previous position. If he was given a broom, he would use this as if it were a Lee-Enfield rifle, and from a stand at ease position he would come to attention, left shoulder arms, take three paces forward, take a left turn, march his hundred paces along the quay, about turn, and march one hundred paces back to his original position, turn to the front, take three paces backwards, drop the broom head to the ground and stand at ease. The odd thing about this eccentricity was his tallying of discharging ship's cargoes was always correct, as listed in the ship's manifest— a phenomenon it was impossible to explain. Anyhow, that's the sort of harmless lunatic Alfie appeared to be.

Now it is a fact that under the "interpretations" of The Dock Workers (Regulation of Employment) Act 1946, there was no such job listed as an OST clerk (OST meaning Overseas Ships' Tally). The job of OST clerk evolved, and was allowed to evolve by the port employers with trade union backing. There is no doubt in my mind, this was a deliberate act, designed to absorb some of the many ex-service officers of the three military services (of whom Alfie was obviously not one) who, having become surplus to

144

military requirements, and being unfit or incapable of doing any skilled trade or professional work, entered the docking industry and formed separate trade union branches from those of the dockers and stevedores, in the Port of London, after World War Two. This was no doubt so as to accommodate, in non-manual employment, a large number of the former members of the Officer Corps.

The recruitment of Registered Port Workers was the responsibility of the National Dock Labour Board, as set out under the Dock Workers (Regulation of Employment) Act. The policy adopted by the trade unions and port employers under the terms of that Act was that port employers would require the National Dock Labour Boards to recruit dockers and stevedores, based on what the port employers considered would be their manpower requirements for the coming year. The National Dock Labour Board would then delegate the responsibility for recruitment to local Dock Labour Boards, in order that they should bring local port registers up to the port employers assumed forward manning requirements.

However, the OST clerical register was always kept at manning levels below the employers stated clerical requirements. This was simply because Registered Ships Clerks were fully aware that, if they were to retain a "full time employment policy" it was better that there should be fewer OST clerks available on the free call, and that dockers who, because of the continuous "over recruitment policy" adopted by the port employers and the Dock Labour Boards', unemployed dockers could then be used to supplement the clerical register, jobs that were usually vested in category "C" men. That then is how I came to be saddled with working with Alfie, the proverbial "nutter" ex-Guardsman, on the day of this tale.

The day began with my being allocated as a "docker-checker" to an Elder-Dempster, West African Coastal Ocean Trading Line. Alfie, the "nutter" OST clerk was already in attendance at his desk in the transit shed, but he was steadfastly refusing to start work until his "stick-man" turned up. A "stick-man" was the general term used to describe "docker checkers" when they were employed to measure packages of cargo that were ready to be loaded aboard a ship.

The stick itself was a four foot in length measure, made up of forty eight one inch marks. Each item of cargo that was to be shipped was measured to the nearest full inch, and each and every measurement of all cargoes for export were recorded together with marks, weights, case, crate or carton numbers, by the OST clerk, onto a "tally pad". The information recorded on the "tally pads" was used first by the "plans man", one of whose jobs was to collect the sheets from the hatch clerks, then enter the items of cargo shown on the tally sheets onto the ship's plan. The ship's plan showed not only at which hatch the individual pieces of freight were stowed, but also in which deck, and where every piece of cargo was in the ship for charging exporting merchants' shipping space.

Once the "plans man" had finished with the tally sheets, they were passed to a "tonnage clerk" who then calculated the weights and/or measurements of all shipped cargo for piece work, ship insurance, and for all other incidental cost related purposes. Therefore the only consolation I had, when I found I had been stitched up to work with Alfie, was that a stick-man's job was non-continuity for dockers, so I only had to put up with working with that scatterbrained, self-indulgent moron, for a single day, hopefully.

As I've stated previously, or if I haven't I meant to explain to the reader, when I turned up in the transit shed, where I was to assist Alfie as his stick-man. He was sitting on a packing case, behind a "shipping off" clerk's desk, haranguing with the ship's gang's pitch hands, and the Port of London's shipping off gang, berating them as to why he wasn't prepared to start work. Of course he wasn't bothered whether he worked or not, because OST clerks were paid on a day-work basis, whereas the dockers were piece workers. When I arrived on the scene, the verbal abuse that had been emulating from Alfie's mouth came to an abrupt end, as he turned his attention on me with the words: 'It's about sodding time you turned up. The lads here have been waiting to start work. They're pieceworkers, or don't you know that. Where the bleedin' hell have you been?'

'In the Dock Labour Compound waiting to be allocated, and if I had known I was to be saddled with you as your stick man, I'd have walked out of the Dock Labour Compound and gone back home.'

'If it wasn't for the fact we know he's a raving nut case, Henry, he'd have been at the bottom of the dock by now. He's had some bleedin' lip to us, he has,' Dave the ship's side ganger said. 'He won't work when he hasn't got a mate, and he won't do a lot when he has. He's a lazy, crazy, bomb-happy, bombastic bastard, that's what he is.'

'Is he trying to insult me?' snapped Alfie.

'Trying? You idiot,' I replied, 'I damn well think he's succeeded. Now that's enough of that, let's get to work. Where's the measuring stick?'

It was near to 8:30 a.m., when we started work. The Port of London wheel-barrowmen began to bring a continual stream of cargo for me to measure, and for Alfie to record onto his tally pad, before it was taken out of the transit shed onto the quay for the ship's pitch hands to make it ready for the crane driver to lift it aboard the ship. Of course, the cargo that came out of the transit shed was used as "topping up freight", that is packages that were used by the ship's loading gang to over-stow heavy cargo that had been pre-loaded from Thames lighters or sailing barges.

In the case of this ship's hold, it had been 1000 tons of "Bulldog Cement" in hundredweight paper sacks, destined for the West African ports of Apapa and Tema, Nigeria. Also, heavy engineering equipment that had been placed in the square of the hatch, with the aid of the ship's own "Jumbo" (Jumbos are a ship's own heavy lift derricks; some ship's were, and possibly still are, specially designed and built to carry heavy lift cargoes. For example: military tanks; inter-continental space rockets; railway locomotives and carriages. Some ships had Jumbos installed that could lift up to 250 tons).

Enclosed docks, such as those in the Port of London, were more like prisoner of war camps than industrial work places. They were all, without exception on the land-side, surrounded by either high brick walls or wooden latticed fences, which reached to a height of between fifteen to twenty feet. There were entrances and exits at strategic places in these walls or fences, to allow motor vehicles, railway goods and passenger trains, and pedestrians, to go about their lawful business—but to do so they had to pass Port Authority policed security boxes that were manned twenty four hours each day. Within these walls and fences it was a man's world; very few women were employed to work there, except in shipping company Head Offices as secretaries or typists. The only other jobs where women worked were in the Port Authority Industrial canteens, and as "mobile van tea ladies." The reason for this was simply because docks were dangerous places to work; they were not places for the meek, weak, squeamish or weary. What's more, not only had they no adequate toilet facilities for dock workers—such facilities for women were absolutely non—existent.

I've had to explain this anomaly simply because dockers and stevedores worked from 8:00 a.m. in the morning, until 7:00 p.m. in the evening—and in many cases all day and all night. The occasion of the mobile tea ladies' arrival at 9:30 a.m. and 2:30 p.m. was always met with jubilation by the quay gangs. This was not simply because tea breaks were the only period throughout the day that many of the men saw a woman to whom they could talk and banter with (some men lived outside the dock perimeter walls and fences, and went home at lunch times), but also because it was a time when they could replenish themselves with food, drink, and rest. Ship's gangs were different, the men rarely came ashore during break periods, choosing to make their own tea aboard ship so as to save time, and get back to work without having to scramble ashore and queue up for food and drink, at the mobile tea vans.

It was a fact that Alfie had a sixth-sense, when it came to the mobile tea van's time to arrive at the transit shed. One could easily tell because he would drop his pencil onto the tally pad and literally bolt out of the transit shed to be in the front of the queue. However, he was always up-staged by the crane drivers working the ship, because it was the excepted practice that crane drivers to the ship's gangs were served first. But this custom and practice never stopped him from trying to "beat the system" simply because, in my opinion, it gave him the excuse to get away from his job of work for as long as possible. After all, he could afford to waste working time; his wages were guaranteed, and not dependent on piecework earnings, as were dockers and stevedores.

The 'mobile tea break' was over and we were returning to work, the ship's side quay gang and me. It was then that I spied Alfie talking to a square box of a man, who had suddenly appeared from under a crane, walking along the quay between the railway tracks towards the dock gates. The stranger was about five feet eight inches tall and almost as broad. He had close cropped hair, and beady blue eyes that were set well into his skull. His arms were short—closer to his hips than to his knees, and when he walked his knees appeared to jerk his lower limbs outwards in a splayed fashion. He looked to be the sort of bloke a wise man wouldn't want to fall out with, but we had to get back to work, the ship's top-hand was bawling from the deck for cargo.

I waved to Alfie, calling out to him to get a move on and to get back to work. But it was at the very least another five minutes before he broke away from the stranger, finally ambling back to his desk as if he hadn't a care in the world.

'Who was that packing case with legs you were talking to?' I asked him.

'Who?' He echoed back at me.

'That bloke you were talking to just now. I've not seen him about the docks before. Where's he from?'

'Oh! Him. That was Bert. He's just come out.'

The barrow-man whose packages I was measuring grimaced and said, 'What's he one of them damn poofters?'

150

'No!' exclaimed Alfie, 'He's just come out of nick (prison). It's the first time I've seen him for years. I hardly recognised him. He's lost quite a bit of weight.'

'What was he in prison for?' I asked.

'Well. He dabbed off in the Dock Labour Compound one day, and went straight home. He found his old woman in bed with the milkman. So, he did no more, he picked the milkman up by the scruff of his neck, and threw him out of the window.'

'What! And he was sent to prison for that? How long did he get?'

'Eight years,' replied Alfie.

'Eight years for throwing a philanderer out of his house. Bit of a harsh sentence that was, wasn't it?' said the barrow-man.

'Well, the milkman was killed, so I don't think that helped Bert's case when it was heard at the Old Bailey.'

'The bloke was killed by being thrown out through a window? How did he manage to get killed doing that? He must have fallen badly?'

'Well. Yes. I suppose he must have. Bert had one of those flats in a new tower block. It was on the seventh floor,' Alfie replied in his usual naive way.

The barrow man shrugged his shoulders in a matter of fact way, stroked his chin, and replied: 'No, I don't suppose it did the milkman a lot of good when he hit the deck in a free fall from the seventh floor, did it? The same thing happened to some of our blokes in the Parachute Regiment during the war, when their parachutes "*Roman Candled*".'

'No,' said Alfie, 'especially when he landed on the spikes of the iron railings, that lined the grass round the bottom of the tower block.'

After that last statement Alfie went quiet, which was a relief to all of us. But I should have known he was concocting some scheme or other, in that demented, cunning brain-box of his. I was soon to find out what it was.

Now as I have already explained, the freight being wheel-barrowed out of the transit shed was for "over-stowing" the cement cargo loaded previously into the ship's "lower-hold" from Thames lighters and sailing barges. It was a job that went on from 8:30 a.m., when I arrived on the scene, until 11:10 a.m. (except for the tea break) when an order came from the ship's deck telling us the ship's gang were about to cover up the lower hold, and that they would be going back "over-side" into a barge to load more "Bulldog Cement" that was to be stowed into the wings of the lower 'tween deck. It was then Alfie said: 'The ship's gang have got 250 tons of cement, that is to be stowed in the lower 'tween deck. It only needs one clerk to tally cement and the gang won't finish loading that until at least five o'clock this evening. I've got a funeral to attend at two o'clock in West Ham cemetery. Do you think I could get away to catch the eleven twenty five train; I should be back by five o'clock, or at least by the time the gang come back ashore.'

I stood thinking about his request for a minute or two. He was, after all, the clerk to the ship's gang. It was his job and responsibility, not mine, to tally (count) the bags of cement, out of the barges into the ship's hold. But as it was for a funeral I told him I would tally the cement. Then, before I could say 'have a jolly funeral', he was off like a bullet,

152

heading along the quay in the direction of Tilbury Town railway station.

Luckily, as it turned out, there was a sudden downpour of rain in the afternoon. It was a thunderstorm that lasted for over an hour. The ship's gang had had to cover up the deck hatchway with a dolly-brook (a large tent shaped canvas) until the rain clouds had passed by. It was after six o'clock when they finally finished loading the cement out of the barges into the ship—that's when Alfie came staggering back along the ship's deck, well inebriated.

'It's about time you came back,' I told him. 'What have you been up to?'

He waved his arms about before he blurted out, 'To a funeral.'

'I know that, you prat,' I said, 'but it doesn't take all bloody day to bury a corpse.'

'Then there was the vake,' he slurred, 'I couldn't mish the vake.'

'The wake, was it an Irish Catholic funeral?'

'Yup, and a bloody fine send-off we gave her, too,' he replied.

'Her! Who was "her"?'

'Bert's ol' woman.'

'When did she die?'

'You won't believe this, but it's as true as I'm standing here,' he said, as he swayed about like a wet flag in a high wind. 'It was the day after Bert came out of the nick.'

'Really?' I said in reply. 'How did she die?'

'Fell, or jumped, out of her flat window. You know, seventh floor up in the tower block. She did the same dive as the milkman had done—and she landed on the same iron railing as the milkman. You would have thought the council

153

had more sense, and had those railings taken down, after the milkman was killed, wouldn't you? It was a case of her falling out of the window, the police seem to think. Though I'm not so sure about that, knowing Bert. It was a very sad affair though. We were all in tears.

She was a nice looking woman she was, too. Bert was especially upset by her death, because he'd made a vow while he was in prison, that when he got out of nick he was going to kill the randy bitch himself. That's probably the reason why she decided to jump out of the window. 'We gave her a good old Irish send-off though, we did,' he said with a slurred voice. Then he said, 'There wasn't a sober man left amongst us, except me.'

'What was Bert's wife's name?' I asked.

'I can't remember,' he replied, as he slumped down on the ship's deck, breathing heavily and dribbling out of the corners of his mouth like a newborn baby, 'Mary, Kathy, something like that. One of those good 'ld Irish names.' Then he muttered, 'It's a lovely cemetery, the Catholic cemetery in West Ham, so it is. I've been and booked my plot there ready for the great day.' Then he said, 'I couldn't bear to think I would be buried amongst you Protestants.'

'What!' I said, 'you cheeky drunken sot. It's all right to have us Protestants doing your work for you all day. But we're not considered by you to be good enough to be buried alongside. Never mind, Alfie. We're all looking forward to your funeral. So tell your wife to get plenty of booze in for *your* wake, because there won't be a docker or stevedore left at work; the docks will have to close down for a day or two, when we all turn up to *see the last of you*.'

However, I need not have bothered to make that speech because Alfie was dead to the world, flat out on the ship's

154

deck, snorting and snoring like a pig basking in the late warm evening sunlight—that's where I left the useless, self-indulgent, drunken sot while I went off to the shipping company's mobile office, to do Alfie's last job of the day. That was to hand in his tally pad and measuring stick to the ships charge clerk, and collect my only means of escape from "bomb-happy" Alfie. That was by drawing my Dock Labour Board Registration attendance book, while hoping to God I wouldn't be allocated to work with him again on the morrow.

Victor and His Embarking Moment

Victor, Vic to us workmates, was a silent man who lived inside himself. Vic could be described as something like a children's Jack in the Box who popped out of his own self-contained mental prison on the odd occasion, when something within him pressed a release button. Then, whatever it was that had bought him out of his box had passed, Vic would pop right back into himself again. This frustrating derangement was, without doubt, his way of coping with whatever was revolving round in the brain cells of his young tormented mind. Yes, Vic was a sad young man, the product of almost six years of torment as a "prisoner of war" in various Stallags in East Germany and Poland. Yes, Vic was a sad young man who worked in the London docklands during the late 1940s and 1950s (after the Second World War) with many other sad young men, men who bore the mental scars of incarceration in prison camps, or of physical scars and battle fatigue of war.

Vic was about five feet seven inches tall (175cm) and scrawny. He had large brown eyes, verging on black, with bright pupils that lit up the irises, possibly due to the medication he had to take for his "Jack in the Box" mental condition. He always wore a peak cap (a form of head gear more commonly known among workmen as a "cheese cutter" because of their sharp brim) to cover the baldness on his oval shaped head, which gave him that "Andy Cap" appearance as depicted in the Daily Mirror cartoons of that period in time—the 1940s, 50s and 60s.

Another of Vic's oddball traits was that he always dressed in heavy clothing; spring, summer, autumn and winter. The only logical explanation that could be found for this curious practice was the years he had spent in those cold north eastern parts of Europe during the Second World War; there could be no other logical explanation than that outlined description of Vic's mental aptitude and personal appearance.

Vic could also be likened to a ghost, for he had the ability to appear and vanish like an apparition; a spectre. For when Vic spoke, which wasn't very often, his voice was soft and low. It was not much louder than a whisper; it was hardly audible even if one was standing close to him. Talking was certainly not one of Vic's strong points. So to put the catalogue of his persona in a nutshell, Victor was one of those people who, when he left one's company, it was as though he had never been there at all; that he had never existed in human form. One could quite easily assume he was merely a figment of one's imagination.

Vic, you see, was a member of the crew of the sinking of the ocean liner "SS Athenia" in 1940, a ship that was torpedoed and sunk soon after the outbreak of the Second World War. He was taken prisoner and spent the rest of the war in German prisoner of war camps in Eastern Europe. He was just fourteen years of age when he was captured, in other words he spent his formative years under constantly armed prison guard scrutiny.

So, it could be said, it was quite possibly during this period of his young life that could explain Vic's somewhat odd behaviour that, on some days, exhibited itself in different eccentric ways; eccentricities that were never exhibited by any other of the war veteran port workers because most of them were suffering from battle fatigue, frustrated by war wounds, or just "bomb happy" from their war service. But just as surely as one lunatic is seen to be mentally normal to any other lunatic, so too is any one "bomb happy" ex-serviceman seen to be mentally normal to any other "bomb happy" ex-serviceman. In fact one could often hear them saying to one another, when they were referring to oneself, 'What's that "bomb happy" sot talking about?'

However, Vic had one major eccentricity that stood out like a sore thumb in his enigmatic prisoner of war shaped character. A habit that none of his contemporaries had acquired during their war service, for he smoked cigarettes he rolled himself, and although that habit in itself was not unusual, he rolled them from tobacco he kept in a battered old tin of dubious origin, that had a Nazi Swastika embossed on its lid, and in which he also kept cigarette papers. What was different about Vic's smoking habit though from the other men who rolled their own cigarettes, was that he had the filthy habit of using the butt (dog ends) of previously smoked cigarettes. He did this by breaking up the butt ends and mixing them with freshly brought tobacco. This thrift was, without doubt, the result of his experiences and privations during his long years in German Prisoner of War Camps.

Now in all docks areas within the Port of London, smoking was prohibited with a fine of two pounds levied on those who dared to flaunt that byelaw. However, to enhance his ability to continue with his smoking habit in these restricted docks areas, Vic used a technique he had perfected some years before, which was to turn a lighted cigarette on his tongue back into his mouth without the aid of his hands. It was a trick he had learnt during his prisoner of war days when in non-smoking areas, or when he contrived to have a smoke unbeknown to his fellow prison inmates. It was now a trick he found useful to employ in the transit shed or on board ships, where smoking was totally prohibited, that is with the exception of three European toilets that had been provided by the port authority in nineteen forty-eight, almost sixty years after Tilbury docks was first opened to shipping. These toilets were sited about half a mile apart for the use of about two thousand dockers, plus lighter-men, OST clerks and lorry drivers.

Now at the time of this tale I was employed with Vic, and fifteen other dockers, as a ship's loading storing gang working on an Orient liner on the southern quay in Tilbury Docks, which in itself isn't such a big deal. However, it may come as a surprise to some readers to learn that a fair proportion of the stewards on this ship were gay, who flaunted and flirted before all and sundry to attract attention. Heterosexuals had to be very careful whom they were dealing with, as ships can be very unsafe places for the gullible and unwary landlubber, but not to an old sailor such as our intrepid Victor P.

Now as I have already explained, Vic was working with a ship's storing gang on an Orient liner that was being prepared for a voyage (actually she was due to sail on an outward bound voyage to Australia). The ship's storing gang had finished putting fresh provisions in the galley for the chef, and they had prepared the bond room ready for customs officers to check the pursers' dutiable stores. That is the recently shipped wines, spirits, cigarettes, cigars and tobacco; before it was sealed, until the ship had sailed clear of British territorial waters, after which the "bond" could be broken open and the "bonded" goods could be released as being free of duty and made available to passengers and crew. So, while the customs officers were checking the bonded goods before the "bond room" was sealed, the stores gang sat around while they waited for orders to commence the next job—that was when Vic vanished to have a smoke with "butt end mixed tobacco" from his Nazi Swastika embossed tin.

Unbeknown to any of his work mates in the stores gang, Vic had made his way up three decks of the ship into the companionway, which served as a thoroughfare between the ship's galley and the stores rooms, where he thought he could have a crafty smoke in peace. However, the companionway was also a strictly non-smoking area, but after being ordered about all his life, sometimes on the wrong end of a prison guard's bayonet, he took little notice of what he was not permitted to do. Vic, you see, had fallen out of love with both convention and authority, especially authority and those who wielded it. He had decided to become his own man.

Now if he wanted to have a smoke—sod them all—he would and he did. Six years of unremitting subjugations was enough, now he was home and free. He had taken his Nazi-embossed tobacco tin from his jacket pocket, unravelled a couple of "dog ends" which he then mixed with some fresh tobacco before rolling the mixture into a cigarette paper. He had lit it when, at that very moment, who should come

160

striding along the deck companionway, none other than Captain Kidd, the shore side Orient Line loading superintendent. Vic's cigarette did an about turn and disappeared inside his mouth without his having to move his hands. At first Captain Kidd walked passed Vic as though he had not seen him, then he suddenly stopped and came striding back. He looked Vic up and down before demanding in a most officious voice, 'Who are you, and what are you doing loitering about here?'

There was no reply from Vic.

'I'm talking to you, my man. Who are you and what are you doing here?'

There was still no reply from Vic.

'Are you deaf?' persisted the Captain, 'Or are you just being stupid? Do you know who I am? I'm Captain Kidd, the Orient Line's superintendent loading officer.'

Vic removed the cigarette from his mouth before saying, 'Thank God for that, Captain. For a minute I thought you were a rent boy soliciting for a customer.'

Then, as Captain Kidd stood with his mouth agape as he contemplated the temerity of this scruff, overdressed individual, Vic slouched slowly and deliberately off down the store's companionway, before vanishing like a ghost among the maze of store deck cupboards, a knack he had obviously picked up during those long years he had spent as a boy prisoner of war in East Germany and Poland. At first you see him—then you don't.

This was when you had pressed a release button. Then, when whatever it was that had brought him out of his box had passed, Vic would pop right back into himself again. This frustrating derangement was, without doubt, his way of coping with whatsoever was revolving round in the brain cells of his young tormented mind. Yes, Vic was a sad young man, the product of almost six years of torment as a prisoner of war in various Stallags in East Germany and Poland. Yes, Vic was a sad young man who worked in the London docklands during the late 1940s and 1950s (after the Second World War) with many other sad young men; men who bore the mental scars of incarceration in prison camps, or of physical scars and battle fatigue of war.

The Prologue
My Last Days as a
Docker/Crane Driver

Before I begin to recount the medical treatments, or to be more explicit the lack of adequate medical treatments, I received from the National Health Service (NHS) following several serious industrial accidents in the docks, it is to first refer back to my previous experiences of hospitalisation prior to the implementation of the National Health Service Act 1948.

I state this as a fact simply because there was no comparison between the medical care I received prior to 1948, when hospitals were run mainly through charitable donations, and that which I received after that date when hospitals became part of a state run welfare apparatus. Doctors acted as agents to, not as employees of, a newly implemented welfare provision, which was designed to provide health care for the whole nation, The National Health Service—a brain child of Aneurin Bevan MP (1897-1960).

This, by the way, is not because I'm an opponent of the National Health Service, far from it. But because of the change in patient care and an attitude that seems to have followed on from a charitable, pre-NHS health care system, supported mainly by donations, and when nursing was considered to be a vocation (a grossly underpaid labour of love by women mainly from the middle class), where doctors received little remuneration for their services, to what it has become today—in too many instances, a money grasping profession.

Before my shipboard accident on board RMS Orion, I had spent over eighteen months in various hospitals during and after the Second World War, due to a farm accident whilst as a child evacuee in Devonshire. That was, of course, before Aneurin Bevan's implementation of the National Health Service Act 1948. He was Minister of Health during the period of post-war administration under the Labour Government (1945-51) during the premiership of Clement Attlee, when hospital services within Great Britain were brought under central government administration.

One example of my pre-NHS experiences was when I was injured whilst evacuated in 1940. I had cut my knee and was attended to by a local GP at his surgery in Totnes. The wound wasn't cleaned, but sewn up with three stitches, the consequence of which was that the wound turned septic. I was taken to Totnes Cottage hospital by a billeting officer, where after an inspection of the injury by the hospital Registrar, I was transferred on to Torbay hospital, Torquay. A Mr Griffith operated and saved not only my leg, but also my life. I spent eight months in Torbay hospital where I was treated with the greatest *loving* kindness by the nurses and doctors, and received the best medical care available at that time (Torbay hospital was set up by the Wills (Tobacco Company) Trust for the benefit of the people of Torbay).

My injury, however, was beyond the orthopaedic skills available at Torbay hospital. In consequence I was first sent to a convalescent home at a place called Tipton St. John, from which I ran away. When I was *recaptured,* and the sister in charge (with the aid of her nursing staff) had failed to encase me in a plaster of Paris cast. I was transferred to Exeter Orthopaedic Hospital, where major surgery was to have been carried out—but fate intervened.

The hospital was already filled with wounded servicemen, from battles in Belgium, France, and at Dunkirk in particular. Then, after that particular influx of military patients had been dealt with, a flood of civilian casualties, from the bombing of Plymouth town, filled the hospital to over-flowing. So, after four months waiting for an operation on my knee, I was discharged as an outpatient back to my pre-accident billet, to await a recall for further treatment. That was an event that never occurred, because I was returned back to my home in Gravesend, Kent. But once again, whilst in Exeter Orthopaedic hospital, I was treated with the greatest kindness, and given the best medical treatment available.

Towards the end of the war, September 1944 to be more precise, my father returned home after spending three years working in the docks in Port Greenock, Scotland, under a "direction of labour order" made by the Dock Labour Corporation. He took me to the Great Ormond Street hospital, London, for an examination of my leg injury. In January 1946 I was admitted into the Royal National Orthopaedic Hospital at Stanmore, Middlesex, where I spent two three-month periods having my leg arthrodeased by a Mr Murphy, under the directions of an orthopaedic consultant, Mr Cholmely. Once again I was treated with respect, and given the best possible medical treatment available at that time.

My next encounter with a hospital was in 1951, when I was rushed into Saint Bartholomew's hospital, Rochester, with peritonitis. I had previously been several times to see my GP, a doctor called Joel, for stomach pains, and had been told by him: 'You may have a grumbling appendix, and it will *probably* go away.'

When the pain did come back with a vengeance, it was a neighbour who was on hand to telephone for an ambulance. I was taken to Saint Bart's Hospital where I was operated on, then spent two weeks in Saint William's Hospital, Rochester, to recuperate after the operation; although it was by then under NHS control. I was treated very well.

My next involvement with a GP, Doctor Joel and the NHS, was when I had a 32 hundred weight set of jute dropped on my foot, while I was working down a ship's hold in Tilbury docks. My foot was black and blue. I could hardly walk on it. I went to see Doctor Joel who, after examining my foot, sent me to Gravesend hospital for an X-ray. On reporting back to Doctor Joel from the hospital, I was told by him, 'There are no broken bones,' then he asked me, 'Where do you work?'

'Tilbury Docks,' I told him.

'Oh,' he replied, 'you dockers don't do much. You may as well go back to work.'

So I was sent back to work in one of the most dangerous industries in the world, by a man who was totally ignorant of what a docker's job entailed. However, God, it's said, works in mysterious ways. My foot got slowly better; Doctor Joel, my NHS GP, dropped down dead a few days after sending me back to work. Who said there's no such thing as justice?

However, my next brush with the NHS was on account of my six-year-old daughter. She was continually having problems with her tonsils, and needed to have them removed. She was referred by our GP to be seen by a consultant at Medway Hospital, Gillingham, Kent, where on the appointed day she was taken by my wife. The consultant pronounced that my daughter would have to join a waiting list, and it would probably be two years before he could operate, but if my wife paid him thirty pounds (twelve to fourteen hundred pounds in today's money value) he could do the operation privately within two weeks. "Christ," I thought when my wife told me this. "Why do I pay National Insurance Contributions?"

I was so angry that I stormed down to my GP's surgery, ready for anything (That was at a time before working class people had telephones; when one could go directly to a doctor's surgery for a consultation or treatment. It was before the advent of patients having to pre-empt the coming of an illness and telephoning a surgery for an appointment or being given an appointment for several days, or weeks, after an illness came on, by which time when one came to see the doctor, one was over the worst of an illness—or had died). But my GP, when I saw him, told me to calm down. He gave me a letter to take to the Charing Cross Hospital, London, and although it was a NHS Hospital, there was no "black-mail" request for money before treatment. The consultant who saw my daughter had her admitted into Charing Cross hospital within two weeks of seeing her, for an emergency operation to remove the seriously infected lymphatic tissue on both sides at the back of her throat. So much for child patient concern by some money grabbing unscrupulous doctors, and similarly unprincipled consultants.

I now have to ask in all honesty, why have we British working class wage slaves allowed ourselves to become saddled with the cost of providing a so called "free health service". A service that costs tax payers billions of pounds per annum to run, and, within which service, certain factions of the medical profession have the temerity to cajole vulnerable patients into paying privately for orthopaedic and surgical operations they are entitled to have carried out at their own expense as tax payers under the NHS. The technique of achieving this transfer of patient care from the NHS to the private sector is simply by threatening to put such patients onto long term waiting lists, if they don't accept the offer to go private.

Can one really believe therefore, it's a Hippocratic Oath that is sworn by newly qualified medical professionals these days, or is it a "Hypocrites Oath"? One has to wonder that when one analyses certain sentences of the oath, e.g. 'I will follow that system of regimen which, according to my ability and judgement, I consider for the benefit of my patients, and abstain from whatever is *deleterious* and *mischievous.*' Also, 'Into whatever houses I enter, I shall go into them for the benefit of the sick, and I will abstain from every voluntary act of *mischief* and *corruption.*'

Unfortunately, the Hippocratic Oath doesn't end with the words, 'So help me, God'. But then Hippocrates was a Greek citizen, living in an era 400 years before the birth of Christ. So, I do suppose he may have had a number of Greek gods of his very own, but I'm sure King Midas wasn't one of them.

My Last Days as a Docker/Crane Driver

I could hear a voice echoing down the lift shaft from far, far away. It appeared to be shouting to no one in particular; yet everyone: 'He's still alive down there, he's still alive.' Then there came the beating of studded boots on steel step plates, as my work mates rushed down through several levels of store decks, and out of the store rooms towards me. I lifted my head and shook it to clear it, my blood slopped about all over the place. *Oh sod it*, I remember thinking, *I've bitten my damn tongue off.*

It was then the steel lift barrier, that acted as a safety barrier for the lift, was crashed open, and an excited voice said, 'Hold on, Henry. We'll soon have you out of there.'

It was then that my docker workmates came into the shattered lift cage, and lifted my battered body off of the aluminium beer drums, on which I was spread-eagled, and carried me into the store-deck companion way; then my brother, who had been working on the quay for the Port Authority, was there with me. Of course, I've always known it to be true that bad news travels fast, and in most cases such news does bring quick results, and the news of this incident was no exception to that rule.

Within a short time of the accident, Port Authority Police Ambulance Officers were in attendance, canvas stretcher opened and ready. They made no fuss about my condition; they'd had plenty of experience of this sort of thing during the 1939-45 War. They quickly had me trussed up securely on a stretcher, then they, my brother and my workmates, began the struggle to lift me up through the narrow store-decks' stairways to the gun-port door, across a narrow gangway onto the dock quay, and secure me into the back of a Port Authority Ambulance. It was then I noticed that both my father and my brother were with me in the ambulance; and that was the last I remembered until I woke up in Tilbury Docks Hospital.

I had been in the Dock Labour Board Compound on the Saturday previous to my accident, with the other members of my ship's gang. We had had no intention of "shaping up" for work, because there was an Orient Liner due to arrive on the following Monday morning, and we were to be the ship's storing gang for the duration of her stay in Tilbury Docks; about ten days of continuous work.

However, just when we thought we were safe from getting tied up with a continuity job, the tannoy system blared out, 'All attendance books into the office', and we knew some of us would be allocated to jobs "up river", or to other docks in the port, or "down river" to load ammunition in the deep water off of Southend, or "off-shore" at Greenhithe to discharge wet or dry pulp. In fact, I was allocated to the East India Docks with Big Dave. The day was Saturday 23rd April 1960.

The East India Docks were difficult to reach, when travelling by train and bus from Tilbury Docks, that is. So, Big Dave and I crossed the Thames from Tilbury Riverside Ferry Terminal to Gravesend, where I had left my old 1933 Austin Seven car. We went via Watling Street, through the Blackwall Tunnel, to reach the East India Docks on the north side of the river. The job we were allocated to was to be part of a ten man ship's quay discharging gang, working on a short-sea trader. We were detailed to act as wheel-barrowmen, trundling boxes of floor tiles and rolls of linoleum from the quay-side into an antiquated transit shed. It turned out to be a well-paying job, however, in so far as we worked all day on the Sunday to finish discharging the ship, a "short sea trader". Fortunately for Big Dave, he was back in Tilbury Docks Labour Compound on Monday morning (25th April 1960) to re-join his own ship's gang to work on a West African Coast Conference cargo-passenger liner.

I, on the other-hand, went to work on the RMS Ship Orion, a pre-1939-45 World War liner of the Orient Line fleet of ships that had operated between Tilbury Docks, Essex and Australia via the Suez Canal for twenty years. That was except for the war years 1939-45, when she was on active service as a troop ship. Then, however, due to the closure of the Suez Canal in 1956, RMS Orion, like all the other ships of the Orient Line and Pacific and Orient Line Fleets, had had to change routes and take the longer passage across the Atlantic Ocean, through the Panama Canal, and across the Pacific Ocean to Australia. That job on the RMS Orion proved to be my last day's work as an 'A' class docker/crane driver.

Having been picked up to work on the RMS Orion, that was berthed at 32 Transit Shed, Tilbury Docks, we members of the ship's store gang made our way to the ship. Our first task on going aboard the vessel was always to remove unwanted empty crates, casks, beer barrels and other disposable paraphernalia, from the store-decks, walk-ways, and the ship's galley. It was put ashore to clear the decks and store rooms, before we began loading the hundreds of tons of victuals for the ship's outward journey. That is meats, fish including caviar, fresh vegetables of every description, soft drinks, beers in bottles tins and drums, wines, cigars, tobaccos, cigarettes, spirits, liquors and more especially whiskey (the wild-wild women for the voyage walked aboard, as fare-paying passengers).

Clearing the store's decks and ship's galley were essential jobs; jobs that had to be completed before the ship began her storing operations. These storing operations had to be completed before the arrival of the ship's deck and engine room crews, whose duty it was to prepare the vessel ready to put to sea and for the stewards to prepare the cabins ready for her passengers when they embarked for the long outward bound journey to Australia.

We had completed discharging all empty and disposable items of the last voyage ashore by breakfast time at 9:00 a.m. Breakfast and lunch was provided for the stores gang by the duty ship's chef, whilst working shore-side, from the ship's galley. Although this practice was unlawful under the Victorian Truck Acts, 1831 and 1887, simply because, 'Every workman is entitled to be paid his wages in cash. Any payment in kind is illegal and void and the value therefore recoverable.' However, this arrangement suited the men of the stores gang who were ignorant of the statutes relating to such employment regulations; but the real reason for this apparent benevolence on the part of the shipping company, was to deliberately detain the stores gang aboard the vessel for the duration of each day's storing operation, a job that extended from 8:00 a.m. until 7:00 p.m. each day, in order that there was continuity in the whole of the storing operations.

It was after we had had our breakfast, in the store deck companion way, that we began to load ten gallon metal casks of beer through the ship's port-side gun-port. The gun-port had a small platform attached to it which, when the gun-port was opened, could be lifted out over the ship's side to receive cargo and stores. Adjacent to the gun-port, on either side of the ship, there were platform lifts, powered by hydraulic

172

rams, which were used by the store-keeper and galley staff to service the ship's bars and the chefs' larders.

It was my job as crane-driver to the ship's gang to operate the lift by the use of a lever outside the lift cage, as well as being responsible for driving a quay crane, or the ship's winches should the need arise. But, as it turned out, fate took a hand. I was helping to stow the beer casks in the lift, when I felt a jerk and surge on the lift wire. 'Get out, Spike!' I yelled to my work-mate, who scrambled out between the lift platform and under the steel safety doors. Unfortunately, I didn't have time to follow him.

The journey down the lift on the runaway platform was so fast that I don't remember any part of it. It was not until I heard a voice echoing down the lift shaft, from what seemed a long distance away, shouting: 'He's still alive down there! He's still alive!' That I realised I was spread out on the bottom of the lift, with my back stretched over the sharp edges of a stainless steel beer cask, while another beer cask crushed my right fore-arm, one my left hand, and my face buried into the side of yet another cask of beer. I had pains in my hand, arm, neck, and right side and back that was excruciating. It was then that I lifted my head and tried to speak, but no sound emerged. I thought I'd bitten my tongue off.

After my father's, my brother's, my work-mates' and the Port Authority police ambulance crews' heroic struggle, to get me out of the stores deck, by literally dragging me up the winding steel stairs into the gun port. I was carried across a precariously narrow 'gangway' before they put me into the back of 'the meat wagon', (as the Port Authority Ambulance was known by the dockers), that was drawn up waiting for me on the quay-side. Then it was a dash round the docks perimeter road to Tilbury Cottage Hospital that was situated outside the Southern Docks vehicle entrance and exit gates.

Tilbury Cottage hospital was a 19th century institution it was built specifically to deal with dockworker casualties, than it was to deal with the then sparse local population. It was one of those obsolescent, ill-equipped hospitals that were taken over by the National Health Service in 1948; and was due for closure and demolition soon after I turned up there as a patient. I can't say I remember much about my visit to that foreboding place. In fact I can't remember having any form of treatment there at all, other than an X-ray. I do remember however, asking my brother through my mangled lips and the gap in my face, where my mouth and teeth had been. If he would go and tell my wife what had happened to me. She was due to have our second child in a few days; I didn't want her upset by some burly police officer going to my home to tell her: 'He won't be home tonight Mrs, he's had a bit of an accident. No, I don't think it's too serious, but I'd keep the Life Insurance Policy handy if I was you.' That, or whatever police officers say when they go to victims' houses to report accidents.

However, I'm sure that soon after I'd arrived at Tilbury hospital, I was given a knock-out injection of some sort, because the next thing I remember was coming to in a ward at Orsett General hospital, some miles away from the docks, with my arm in plaster, and my face sewn up from the bottom of my chin to the top of my nose, and a voice close by saying, 'Who is it, Ron?'

And Ron replying, 'It's Henry, I think?'

Then the first voice saying something like, 'Christ! Is it? I'd never have recognised him.'

When some time later I was showed my face in a mirror, neither did I recognise me (for the record, over half of the patients in the ward were injured dockers in various states of physical disrepair; fractured arms, legs shoulders and spines, plus an amputee, or two).

The day following my accident, the male charge nurse and his male staff nurse came to my bed.

'You can get up and sit in the bedside chair,' they told me.

'I can't move,' I replied through my patched up swollen lips. Lips that, although not stitched together, nonetheless restricted my speech. 'I've got pains in my back, my neck, my right wrist, my left hand and right side. If you want me up, then you'll have to get me up.'

Without any more ado, they proceeded to roll back the bedclothes. Then, with each of them grasping an upper arm, they literally yanked my battered, broken and badly bruised body out of bed, and dropped me in a bedside chair.

I have no idea how many hours I had been in bed, propped up with pillows and a backrest. It was obvious to me, when I came to, that I'd been operated on. Because my right arm was encased in plaster of Paris and my face was stitched up from the top of my nose to the underside of my chin. But when I was yanked out of bed, my shoulders were rounded with my head pointed towards the ward floor. I must have looked like the Hunchback of Notre Dame when I was lifted up to walk the following day by two physiotherapists. My back and neck, I told them, were giving me hellish pain, so after my walk-about, a diet of pain killing tablets was prescribed, something like two three times a day. No doubt this was to act as a *cure all* for all my injuries.

The charge nurse, who for the record was a Yugoslavian displaced person, told me in his broken English, 'Except for your wrist and face, there are no other apparent injuries, so you will be going home in a few days.' Instead, however, on the following day, I was taken back down to the operating theatre, where my damaged right wrist was reset. It had apparently been wrongly set after the accident.

I should mention here that before they got me out of bed, some bloke came to see me. He introduced himself as being a Board of Trade Officer, and asked me if I could remember how the accident had happened. I told him, 'I was in the ship's store lift, level with the port-side gun-port door, loading drums of beer. Then I was at the bottom of the lift shaft, spread out over the drums of beer.' He got up and walked off; I never saw or heard from him again.

As it turned out it was a forlorn hope on the charge nurse's part, my being discharged that is, because on the 28th of April, the day my son was born, I was hobbling along the ward when I was confronted by the male staff nurse (the male charge nurse was on a day's leave).

'Why,' the staff nurse demanded to know, 'don't you stand up straight and walk properly? Mr Pearce, the Orthopaedic Surgeon who you're under, has pronounced you fit except for your wrist and facial injuries.'

Up till that time I hadn't, to my personal knowledge, seen or been seen by a Mr Pearce. I was so angry (primarily because I already had a stiff right knee that was due to an injury I had received when I was evacuated as a child during the Second World War; an injury that caused me to limp), because this so-called "angel of mercy" had the gall to infer

I was "swinging the lead", so I told him, 'The next person to tell me to "stand up and walk properly" is going to get this plaster of Paris covered arm straight in their mouth!'

He was actually taken aback and told me, 'Go and sit by your bed. I'll have a word with the hospital registrar.'

Shortly after this verbal exchange, the male staff nurse came down the ward and told me to walk to the x-ray department. Then, after having had an x-ray of my spine, and shortly after returning to the ward, the staff nurse came down the ward again, somewhat tongue in cheek I thought, and said, 'You will have to go back to the X-ray department, the radiologist thinks he may have detected an injury.'

I started to walk off down the ward, but the staff nurse called me back and told me, 'Get up on your bed, the hospital porters will be here in a few minutes.'

Very soon after this, two porters came with a trolley onto which they lifted me, having refused my offer to get on the contraption myself. I was then wheeled back down to the x-ray department for an encore with the x-ray machine; after which I was lifted back onto the trolley, wheeled back to the ward, gingerly lifted back onto my bed, and advised by the staff nurse, 'You have two suspected fractures of the spine, at the 4th and 5th lumber vertebrae, but the radiologist,' he assured me, 'isn't positive about this, because the x-ray machine isn't very good.' Orsett General Hospital was a relatively new hospital at that time, with new medical equipment including x-ray machines.

Then I asked the male Staff Nurse, 'Could you get a dentist to extract a tooth from under my nose? I've asked you before about this, and you've taken no notice.'

He said nothing, but later that day a dentist came to the side of my bed, pulling out a small x-ray machine. He said, 'You think your front tooth is under your nose, so I understand. What makes you think that?' Or similar words to that effect.

'Because I can feel it there, that's why,' I replied.

He said no more, but got on with the job of taking an x-ray, he then walked off to get it developed. When he returned he said in a somewhat surprised manner, 'You were right, you've got an incisor tooth wedged up under your nose, and a gap where two premolars had been before the accident, I'll have to extract that incisor. There are two molars that are also loose and they shall have to be extracted at a later date.' Then he said not another word, but drew the curtains round the bed and gave me a whiff of gas. When I had regained consciousness, the dentist had gone, and so had the large lump that had been pushing one side of my nose out beyond my sewn-up top lip.

So it was on 28th April 1960, on the day my wife gave birth to our son, and three days after my accident aboard the RMS Orion. I was confined to my hospital bed for 28 days, with suspected fractures of the 4th and 5th lumbar vertebrae. However, each evening at visiting time during that month, a docker from the various gangs would call in to see me. Each of them brought with him a little gift which he would shove into my bedside locker. I discovered, when they got me out of bed, that the packages contained little bags of silver coins they had collected between the gangs. Believe me, I've never forgotten that unsolicited kindness, nor shall I—ever.

On the day after I was got out of bed, and five weeks after my admission into Orsett Hospital, I was discharged. I was taken by Bill Bloss, one of my docker workmates, by motor car to Tilbury Riverside Passenger Terminal. Orsett Hospital, for reasons best known to its management, had refused to provide transport for me. Bill Bloss put me onto one of the passenger river boat ferries, to be transported back to Gravesend. My brother was waiting by the ferry terminal to take me home, where my wife, my daughter and my month-old baby son were waiting, no doubt in trepidation, to greet me.

I've no idea what my family thought of me, as I walked in through my front door with a newly healing scar running from the bottom of my chin to the top of my nose, a front and two side teeth missing, with my arm still lashed up in plaster of Paris, bent over like a hunchback, and dragging my stiff leg along as though it was attached to a leg iron. But for my part, I was more than pleased to be back in my own home to be with my wife and family. Battered though as I certainly was, traumatised too, with bouts of depression and fits of violent temper to follow, due to the pain from my many injuries, most of which were not included in the hospital's medical records.

However, that was not the end of this saga as it turned out, but only the end of the beginning of my many months of negative medical treatment, under the swearing of the Hippocratic Oath profession that worked within the National Health Service. So help me God, I'd had such faith in the medical profession before my accident. That faith had quickly evaporated with my treatment at Orsett General Hospital, and even more so with the treatment I was to receive at the hands of the next lot of orthopaedic, medical, and physiotherapist practitioners at St Bart's Hospital, Rochester, Kent. I had been transferred to St Bart's Hospital, from Orsett General Hospital, because it was the closest

NHS hospital to my home. That was a decision I was painfully to come to regret, for the rest of my natural life.

So it was in June 1960, that I was taken by ambulance from my home, to be seen by a Mr Epps at St Bart's Hospital, Rochester. There was no examination as such, or x-rays taken. I have to admit that I have no knowledge as to whether Mr Epps had received my medical records from Orsett Hospital. He did ask me how I had come by my accident, but he appeared not to be too interested. He had, quite possibly, heard far too many stories similar to mine. After all, St Bart's was the casualty reception hospital for those registered stevedores who worked the shore and shipboard operations on the river Medway. The Port of Medway had the unenviable record at that time, of having the highest casualty rate of any port in the country, with between 20% and 25% of its work force suffering major injuries each year.

I explained to Mr Epps about the pains in my wrist, neck, back, right side and left hand, but his main interest appeared to be in my right wrist. He ordered the removal of the plaster of Paris that had been applied at Orsett Hospital, and ordered that I should attend the occupational therapy department under a Miss Dunn, a Miss Payne and a Mr Pink, to 'get your wrist moving'. Back exercises in the gymnasium under a Mr Wilson, a former Petty Officer Physical Training Instructor in the Royal Navy, traction for my neck injury in the physiotherapy department, and he further ordered that I should attend a Doctor Hicky's clinic.

As I have previously stated, no further x-rays were taken at St Bart's Hospital, even though I had explained to Mr Epps where the areas of pain were located. Nor were any tests carried out, other than by a Doctor Hicky, whose sole contribution to what can only be termed a farce, was to stick rows of pins into my left arm and trace between them with a colouring pen. No! It wasn't acupuncture. It was, so I was informed, a method of tracing to determine if there was any damage to my nerves.

My treatment in the occupational therapy department consisted of printing invitation cards on an antiquated hand press, under the direction of a Miss Dunn, and a Miss Payne, sawing up lengths of wood to make a small table from timber that had previously been a bedside ward locker, under instruction by Mr Pink, an occupational therapist. In the gymnasium, a Mr Wilson, the physical training instructor, had me climbing up and hanging down from wall bars, and throwing a medicine ball about. In the physiotherapy department, I received neck traction. Incidentally this was the only part of any treatment that gave me some relief from my neck and back pain. This charade continued until November 1960, when I was told I was fit enough to return to dock work. So, I had to borrow £400 from my father to buy a vehicle, to convey me from my home in Strood to West Street, Gravesend. That was where I could catch a ferry boat to Tilbury Riverside Ferry Terminal, and then get a bus to take me close to Tilbury Dock Labour Compound.

Mr Epps told me he had written to the London Dock Labour Board Manager, asking that I should be given a light sedentary job. Although why he should have concerned himself is a mystery to me, considering he was apparently of the opinion I was shamming my injuries.

My first job back in the docks was a general run of the mill operation. I was allocated by the Dock Labour Board Manager, together with seven other dockers, five of whom had just returned to the docks for light duties after being injured. We were to act as a ship's quay loading gang allocated to work for the Port of London Authority. Our job was to wheel-barrow bales of periodicals (known as gootches by us dockers) from a transit shed to a ship's side, where the ship's gang's "pitch-hands" prepared them to be lifted aboard the ship by crane.

The bales weighed six hundredweight each (305 kilograms) and we were a returned gang of injured dockers—a gang that was comprised of: two men who had received fractures of the spine and other injuries from falling down ships holds; two men who had received fractured shoulder blades and other injuries, also from falling down ships' holds; one man who had had his leg broken from being struck by a set of cargo whilst working in a ship's hold; and one man who had lost a leg, having had it crushed by a bale of coconut fibre, whilst working in a Thames lighter on a discharging ship. The leg had been so badly damaged it had to be amputated. The other two members of the gang were 'B' men, that is to say they were over sixty five years of age. They were the only two *fit* men in the gang!

Of course, I wasn't in a fit physical state to return to dock work, and had to continually have time off. But on 28th April 1961 (my son's first birthday), I received a letter from Mr Epps' secretary, a Mrs E. K. Cook, asking me to attend his clinic on 8th May 1961 '... for an examination in connection with your accident claim, at the request of your solicitor: Messrs George Hill Goulstone & Co., *Solicitors & Commissioner for Oaths, 25 John Street, Bedford Row, London, W.C.1.*'

Mr Epps was his usual self at this examination: pert, self-assured but distant. I had no idea what he wrote down, only that his report was taken directly from my hospital notes, but with no input from me. In fact, he hardly spoke to me at all.

I was, in reality, superfluous to the so-called examination process. The whole examination and interview were over in no more than 15 minutes, as he flicked through the notes and took a cursory look at my arm, before I was dismissed. As far as I could make out, Mr Epps had already made out his report and signed and sealed it, ready for his medical secretary to prepare it for my solicitor's perusal.

Several weeks later I received a letter from Mr Goulstone, asking me to come to his office, to discuss the Epps Medical Report. To say the very least, the report virtually stated there was nothing wrong with me, other than I had 'scarring of face and loss of three teeth, fracture dislocation of right wrist, chip fracture of L1', and that (in his professional opinion) I was suffering more from 'compensation neurosis' than from my injuries. This report was written by a NHS consultant orthopaedic surgeon, with a FRCS after his name.

D. J. Foley, the newly appointed Tilbury Docks London Dock Labour Board Welfare Officer made it his business to meet me. Dan, I have to point out, was something different when compared to previous Dock Labour Board Welfare Officers, all of whom were formally employed as Registered Dockers. He actually cared for the registered dock workers' health and welfare. He had been a docker himself, and had lost a leg working in the docks. He most certainly knew the score when it came to "quackery", for he had obviously suffered from a dose of it himself. My first meeting with Dan was when I was ordered to return to work after one of my progressive bouts of pain in my spine, neck and right side. I had taken a certificate from my GP to the Dock Labour Board Office, handed it to a clerk and waited.

Dan came to the window, looked me straight in the eye for a few seconds, he then said, 'Dilated pupils. You don't look at all well to me, taking a lot of pain killers, are you? Come into my office.'

When I'd entered his office and had sat down he said, 'Have you any idea what is on this certificate?'

'No,' I replied, 'my GP sealed it in an envelope.'

'Yes, he did,' said Dan. Then he said, 'You don't look at all well to me. How do you feel in yourself?'

'I think I'm dying,' I told him, 'I'm in constant pain. I've clued things up as much as I can for my wife, but I think I've had it.'

'Are you a member of the Industrial Orthopaedic Society, The Manor House Hospital?' he asked.

'No,' I replied.

Dan got up without saying another word, walked into the main LDLB office, and when he returned he simply said, 'You are now. Go straight back home and report to your doctor, I'll be telephoning him. If he won't give you a certificate to be off work, don't worry. I'm going to arrange for you to be seen by the resident surgeon at Manor House Hospital for a full examination. I will contact a solicitors' firm, Messrs George Hill Goulstone & Co., to advise George of your case, and of my intention to have you thoroughly medically examined before you are allowed back here to work. I know George Goulstone personally. I shall ask him to contact you as soon as is possible. He will, no doubt, want a copy of any medical report from the Manor House Hospital. On your way back, go to your GP's surgery. After you've seen him, go straight home. Wait until you get an appointment to go to Manor House Hospital. Go on. Go home.'

184

I left Dan's office to wend my way slowly back to Tilbury Riverside Ferry Terminal, about half a mile from the LDLB office. I had to walk because the LDLB office was in the docks, and the distance between the office and Tilbury Docks Railway Station outside the dock's perimeter fence was about the same. By the time I had reached the riverside ferry terminal though, dragging my stiff leg with its invisible ball and chain, I was all in. My only consolation was I had my new Austin van close by the Gravesend ferry terminal, waiting to take me home.

The encounter with my GP at his surgery was brief. He was reluctant to issue me with another certificate to be off work, but he did. Quite obviously Dan had had a word in his ear over the telephone. Immediately after my GP's verbal diatribe relating to my audacity to request a further "off work certificate", I telephoned Dan from a public call box (we working class people could not afford telephones of our own those days), and told him what had transpired between my GP and myself. He said, 'Don't worry yourself about that. I've contacted George Hill Goulstone, your solicitor. He has been in touch with Manor House Hospital. Arrangements are being made for you to be seen by the resident surgeon, Mr J. W. Nicolson, and a Dr Hadley of the Shipping Federation.

'Would you please attend Manor House Hospital on Wednesday, 29th March 1961 at 3:00 p.m. to be seen by Mr J. W. Nicolson and a Dr Hadley, at the request of Messrs George Hill Goulstone & Co., for a full medical report on your injuries and medical condition.'

The medical report by Mr J. W. Nicolson, MB, CH. B. FRCS, was in stark contrast to the one that was concocted by Mr Epps, FRCS. I suppose that was because x-rays were taken at Manor House Hospital which, together with a full and as near as possible comprehensive examination by Mr Nicolson and Dr Hadley, in preparation for a medical report for Messrs George Hill Goulstone & Co. representing me, and Dr Hadley for the Shipping Federation. Unfortunately, the x-rays did not show the fractures to the 4th and 5th lumber vertebra.

It wasn't until 1990, thirty years after the shipboard accident on the RMS Orion, that a scan of my lumber spine was taken at 26 Harley Street, London, on behalf of the Manor House Hospital. X-rays once again showed the fractures of the 4th and 5th lumber vertebra, which by that time were causing me great pain and physical distress. Tests also showed the injuries to my right side, which a previous angiogram and pyelogram tests carried out at Gravesend and North Kent Hospital at the behest of my GP, Dr Beatrice James did not bring to light. These tests showed I had a crushed kidney caused by the impact of the fall in the ship's lift when I landed right side down onto stainless steel beer barrels in the ship's lower stores deck.

However, after my medical examination at Manor House Hospital on the 29th March 1961 and the obvious variation between the medical reports of Mr Epps, Mr Nicolson, and Dr Hadley, George Hill Goulstone, on the 24th April 1961, sent a copy of Mr Nicolson and Dr Hadley's report to Mr Epps at St Bart's Hospital. Another copy of that report was given to me to take to my GP. My GP had a nervous twitch in his left eye that speeded up when he was agitated. After he had read the report, his nervous twitch began to flap his eyelid up and down like a Royal Naval signal lamp. Then he said, 'Who wrote this rubbish?' He turned to the back page of the report and gasped.

I didn't wait to find out what his further reaction to the medical report was, but it ended my association with that GP's practice and St Bart's Hospital. Because on my next visit to St Bart's I was signed off by a Dr Hickey to return to work in the docks. My days of employment as a docker/crane driver were ended, due to the severity of my injuries. The LDLB manager then had me re-categorised as a grade 'C' docker.

On my returning to work at the docks, my physical condition continued to deteriorate, even with the vast quantity of pain killing tablets I had been prescribed to take. However, things began to change after I received a letter from Manor House Hospital to attend Mr Nicolson's clinic for a second medical examination, at the request of my solicitor and the Shipping Federation. The medical examination took place on 4th September 1961 by Mr Nicolson, with Dr Hadley of the Shipping Federation in attendance. Dr Hadley was there to represent the Shipping Federation that was the insurer to The Port of London Master Porters and Stevedores, who were my employers at the time of the shipboard accident. This led once again to Dan, the London Dock Labour Board Welfare Officer at Tilbury Docks contacting Manor House Hospital, and my subsequently being given an appointment to attend Mr Nicolson's clinic for a consultation, with a view to seeking further treatment for my injuries, now that St Bart's had discharged me as being fit for work.

On having been examined by Mr Nicolson at Manor House Hospital, I was referred on by him to be seen by Mr J. R. Armstrong, a visiting consultant orthopaedic surgeon to the Manor House Hospital. The appointment was made for Wednesday 9th August 1961. Mr Armstrong immediately arranged that I should be hospitalised for treatment. I was admitted into Ward 4 at Manor House Hospital on 11th September 1961, where the ward was overseen by sister Puddy, an Australian nurse of sensitive but strong character, and where I stayed as an in-patient until 14th November 1961 for treatment for those many injuries I had sustained on 25th April 1960.

When I arrived in Ward 4 I got quite a shock; the whole ward was filled with workmen from different heavy industries throughout the country: iron foundries, steel works, the railways, ship-yards, coal mines etc.– all of whom had received the same sort of medical dereliction as myself. And there was I, beginning to think I was suffering from paranoia. The medical profession, as exemplified by National Health Service staff, didn't just hate dockers as I'd come to believe, and me in particular. But it appeared they disliked all working class men, anyone that is who contributed towards paying their salaries or wages through National Insurance contributions and taxes. Christ, you can't believe what a relief that was to me, not being the only victim of medical negligence, or just plain indifference to work-peoples injuries, their pain and suffering.

Of course, the assessments of medical professionals did not end with industrially injured victims' discharge from hospital. It spilled over into the legal field, where compensation for loss of faculty became a major issue. More especially when it also brought about loss of future wage earnings. In my case, as in countless others, it has to be pointed out that by my having been injured at work, I was entitled to be compensated through the National Insurance (Industrial Injuries) Act of 1946, as well as making a common law claim through the courts for my injuries.

The Industrial Injuries Act was, and still is, a Contributory Act, whose recipients are paid from funds raised by wage deductions and employer contributions, as laid down under 2.—(1), Part 1, Chap 52 of the National Insurance Industrial Insurance Act, 1946, while the Assessment of Extent of Disablement is to be found under Schedule 4 of that Act. So, Industrial Injury Benefits are *not* based on national charity, as many people are mistakenly led to believe, but on deductions from employed earnings.

'The disabilities to be taken into account, caused by an industrial accident, shall be all disabilities (whether or not involving loss of earning power, or additional expense) to which the claimant may be expected, having regard to his physical and mental condition at the date of the assessment, to be subjected during the period to be taken into account.'

In my particular case, the injuries stated by the Medical Board that examined me on 21st November, 1960, found the conditions to be taken into account were: scarring of face and loss of teeth, fracture dislocation of right wrist, chip fracture of L1, contributing factor stiff right knee from a previous injury.

This assessment was, no doubt, based on the medical records held at St Bart's Hospital (records that had vanished when a request was made for them some time later). In fact, subsequent medical evidence showed my injuries from the accident of 25th April 1960 to have been: fracture of 4 & 5 lumber vertebra, L1 and crushed coccyx; damaged cervical spine; fracture of right scaphoid (the injury never united); broken nose, facial lacerations with 32 stitches required through the nose, lips and upper jaw; three teeth knocked out at the time of the accident, two teeth removed after the accident; damage to both hips, left knee and cervical spine (right hip replaced in 2001) 'due to considerable jarring' caused by the fall; crushed kidney due to falling onto beer drums through three decks of the RMS Orion.

Under the National Insurance (Industrial Injuries) Act, all injuries (as shown above) were entitled to be taken into account by Medical Boards and/or Medical Tribunals. And although I have been before a number of these boards, never once have all my known injuries been taken into account.

After my treatment under the NHS and in stark contrast, the Industrial Orthopaedic Society's Manor House Hospital was a God-send. Mr Armstrong, the visiting consultant orthopaedic surgeon, soon laid down a regime of treatment and aids that put me back on my feet. After my discharge from Manor House Hospital, I was seen regularly by Mr Armstrong every three months, then on his retirement by a Mr Candlin, until finally the injuries to my spine worsened and a scan at 26 Harley Street finally again exposed the fractures to my 4th & 5th lumber vertebra. I was hospitalised in Manor House Hospital, where an epidural and other treatment was administered to my lumber spine. Dan Foley, the Tilbury Docks Dock Labour Board Welfare Officer, would never let go of my case. He was of the opinion from the first time we met, that I'd been short changed by NHS consultants, Medical Boards and Medical Tribunals, but he was aware decisions were based on medical evidence provided by NHS hospitals and GP patient records.

After the experience with my former GP, I change to another medical practice, where the doctors were more like family friends. It was due in no short measure to the professionalism of Dr Colin Smith, Dr Muller, Dr Beatrice James and Dr Carman, that my other injuries from the shipboard accident were diagnosed and I finally received medical treatment. The treatment being carried out through the good offices of the Industrial Orthopaedic Society at Manor House Hospital, North End Road, Golders Green, London, NW11 by specialists such as the late Sir John Nicolson, MB., CH. B., FRCS., Mr Neil Painter MS, FRCS, FACS, Mr K. Maruthappu, MB, FRCS, the resident surgeons, and Mr J. R. Armstrong, MS, FRCS, Mr Candlin, FRCS, and Mr Etheridge, visiting consultant surgeons.

On the 1st May 1962, I received a telegram that read: Case in List for Tomorrow, Tuesday. Be at High Court Strand London; Court No 9 9:45 a.m. sharp = Goulstone.

When I arrived at the Law Courts in London, I was met by Mr George Goulstone and a Mr W. R. Rees-Davies QC., MP who had been briefed to act as my counsel (for the record, Mr Rees-Davies had only one arm. He'd mislaid the other one during the Second World War on some battlefield or other. So he had my case papers tucked up under his elbow in the same way that "No Neck's" father, "One Arm", held his OST Clerk's ships papers down in the docks. At least, I thought, I've got counsel acting for me who has some experience of disability).

After a short discussion, when I was informed by Mr Rees-Davies that the other side had offered a full and final settlement of £2,000, which I rejected (I was in debt to more than that through back mortgage repayments and money I had borrowed from my father to buy a van to get me back and forth to work). Rees-Davies and George Goulstone walked off to haggle with a couple of legal beavers, who were acting on behalf of the Shipping Federation. When they came back, Rees-Davies advised me they had raised their offer to £3,300 that Rees-Davies advised me to accept. We then had to go into Court Number 9 to wait on a Mr Justice

Widgery for the case to be put before the learned judge for settlement that was the amount of damages to be paid together with the costs.

While waiting for my case to be concluded, I sat in Court Number 9 and listened to a case that was in progress. Really, I couldn't believe my ears. A doctor was in the witness box being cross-examined. The questioning went something like this:

Counsel: 'Now, Doctor X. Your patient, Mr Y came to your surgery complaining he had hurt his back?'

Doctor X: 'Yes, he did.'

Counsel: 'Did Mr Y explain to you how he had come to hurt his back?'

Doctor X: 'Yes. He told me he had been lifting a twelve-gallon churn of milk onto the back of his lorry, whilst standing on a wooden box. He said the box had broken, causing him to land heavily and jar his back.'

Counsel: 'What treatment did you prescribe for your patient?'

Doctor X: 'I put him on a course of DF-118s and gave him a certificate to be off work for two weeks.'

Counsel: 'To what purpose, Doctor?'

Doctor X: 'The DF-118s were to relieve the pain, and two weeks off work for the injury to settle down.'

Counsel: 'What treatment did you recommend, when Mr Y returned to your surgery, still complaining of back pain?'

Doctor X: 'I advised him to go back to work, the exercise would do him more good than taking DF-118s and sitting about brooding.'

Counsel: 'You didn't think of sending Mr Y to hospital for an x-ray. Why?'

Doctor X: 'In my opinion, Mr Y was shamming injury.'

Counsel: 'Really, Doctor! So, when you told Mr Y he could go back to work, what did the deceased say to you?'

The learned judge, who had been sitting on his lofty perch with one eye half closed, apparently bored out of his life with the cross examination, sat up sharply, 'Am I led to understand,' he addressed his remark to counsel, 'that Doctor X's patient died from his injuries?'

'That, your lordship, is what we are here to determine,' counsel replied.

I sat shaking my head in disbelief. Is this all that we common working class men can expect from the medical profession, when we suffer injury at work? What is the motive for their actions? Is it part of a conspiracy to deny working men the right to seek compensation? Oddly enough, what went through my mind was a remark supposedly made by a highwayman with the same surname as my own. A John Bradford, a couple of centuries before, when a fellow highwayman was dragged off to be hanged. For he is reputed to have been heard to say, 'There, but for the grace of God, go I.' I thought yes! Amen to that.

The Epilogue

Doubt it not, for even I would not have had the temerity, or the blind arrogance, to have believed the tales I've written about, or am about to unfold had not the hospital medical records, medical boards and medical tribunals records relating to these incidents still be extant to prove the facts of this disgraceful episode of my treatment under some National Health Service medical practitioners.

However, the jobs of dockers and stevedores were, as too were many other heavy manual work operation throughout industry (especially coal mining operations) extremely dangerous work occupations. I for one was injured a number of times during my docking and clerical working days in the docks, both aboard ships and ashore in transit sheds. Thankfully, due to Dan, our London Dock Labour Board Welfare Officer, most of my injuries were treated at Manor House Hospital through the Industrial Orthopaedic Society, but on some occasions this could not always be possible, simply because of the circumstances, as the following cases are testament to.

The date was 2nd June, 1970. I had only recently returned to work in the docks, after having successfully completed a Works Study Practitioners Course, sponsored jointly by The National Ports Council for the Port Transport Industry and the South West London College.

I had been detailed to work as the OST clerk to a ship's gang that was loading cases of KDCCs (a term that meant knocked down case cars). As I was taking down the details of a case that was about to be hoisted aboard a ship, I was struck across the face by a piece of loose timber that had been catapulted at me when the crane driver took the weight of a set of cargo, ready to lift it onto the ship.

Of course, I had no idea what had struck me. I was knocked by the force of the blow from the quay into the transit shed, but I was fully aware that blood was pouring from my nose. The crane driver came down from out of the crane cabin, and with the pitch hands tried stemming the flow of blood, but to no avail. I was taken to the London Dock Labour Board's Medical Centre, where a nurse laid me down on a bunk and applied cold compressions to the injury. Then she told me, 'When you get home tonight, if the injury is still bleeding, go to your nearest local hospital for treatment.'

When I arrived home my nose was still leaking blood, so I made my way to the Medway Hospital, Gillingham, Kent. I booked in at the out-patients department, and waited the usual couple of hours of purgatory, while waiting to be seen by a doctor. When a young white-coated apparition finally made its appearance, it lifted the end of my nostril with some form of instrument, proclaimed that there was no apparent damage other than to the mucous membrane, told me the bleeding would eventually stop, and discharged me.

The following day when I went to work, I went to see my employer's labour manager, and explained what had happened relating to the accident, and that my shirt had been torn, covered in blood, and would the firm be prepared to buy me a replacement shirt.

'Where's the shirt?' he'd asked.

'In the dustbin,' I'd replied.

'No shirt, no replacement,' he said.

'Is that so?' I'd told him, 'I'll have a word with Dan about that.'

I left my visit to Dan Foley, the Welfare Officer for the London Dock Labour Board, Tilbury Docks, for about a week. By the time I got to see him I could hardly breathe through my nose; I was snorting like a pig.

'What's wrong with your nose? It sounds more like the noise from a pig's snout,' he said.

I explained to him what had happened. He rubbed his index finger and a thumb down the sides of my nose. Then he said, 'You've got a broken nose. Call in to your doctor's surgery and get your GP to write a letter for you to attend Manor House Hospital, they'll sort it out.'

Acting on Dan's advice, I got a letter from my doctor which I sent to Manor House Hospital. In a few days I received an appointment date to attend the surgery of a Mr Etheridge, the ENT (ears, nose and throat) specialist at the Manor House Hospital. Mr Etheridge was a large, robust man and blunt as an unsharpened carving knife.

'What appears to be the bother?' he asked.

'I'm having trouble breathing through my nose,' I told him.

'Hum. Let's have a look,' he said, and promptly shoved a tool into my nostril and looked into it. 'It looks all right to me, but you'd better go and get it x-rayed.'

When I'd returned to his surgery, Mr Etheridge said, after perusing the x-ray plate, 'Did you know you had had your nose broken before?'

'No, but I had my nose cut in half in a dock accident in 1960,' I told him.

'That's when it happened by the look of it,' he said, 'And how did you get *this* broken nose?'

I explained what had happened on the day of the accident.

'Oh, really! You'll sue the bastards, won't you?'

'I don't know. I'll ask Dan Foley, our dock Welfare Officer, what he advises.'

'Yes, I know Dan. You tell him from me that I'll write a medical report to whomever he nominates to take on your litigation. I worked down in the docks on and off during my student days. Bloody port employers, you sue the bastards.' Then he said, 'You'll have to come in to have that nose operated on. I'll get my secretary to give you a date. I'll see you then, but you won't see me,' and he gave a sort of snorted laugh.

So it was on the 5th December 1970 that Mr Etheridge had me in Manor House Hospital to successfully re-assemble the bones in my nose. It was a week later, on the 11th December 1970 that I returned home. When I went back to work in the docks, I went to Dan's office. He looked at me and said, 'That nose job Etheridge did on you has improved your looks no end, even those scars from that shipboard accident have almost disappeared.' He laughed and said, 'By the way, I've spoken to our legal friend, George Hill Goulstone, about your accident. He wants to see you to talk about the case. I'll let him know you're back in circulation, and he'll write to you, OK?'

So as not to leave you in the dark, I was awarded six hundred pounds compensation for my injury; these included "special damages". Of course, I was not privy to what

George Hill Goulstone received by way of legal fees, or what Mr Etheridge may have got for preparing a medical report. What I do know is the refusal by the labour manager simply to pay for a new shirt by the shipping company, must at that time have been one of the most expensive shirts in the world.

Now, as if that experience wasn't bad enough, thirteen years later I was involved in a road accident on my way home from work. I had been working during a morning shift on 31st January 1983, for Port Documentation Services Limited on the Southern Berths, West African Terminal, Tilbury Docks, Essex as the second customs clearing clerk. The customs clearing clerk's job also entailed some secondary duties, one of which was to assist Port Health Inspectors where documents were required from HM Customs for cargo clearance purposes.

Prior arrangements had been made for the 31st January for port health inspectors to carry out inspections of a number of containers of imported meat products from West Africa. As port health inspectors work to their own time schedule and also because of the state of the weather as it may have affected the perishable cargoes, it was thought by all concerned that we should work on, despite the weather conditions, to complete the cargo's inspection, and re-seal the containers so that the delivery of the imported merchant's perishable freight could be transported on to the owners, as soon as was possible.

After the examination by the port health inspectors of the containers' contents, the re-sealing of the containers and the HM Customs clearance documentation had been completed. We ships clerks, who had been involved on that particular job, were given permission by the company's charge clerk to proceed home.

It was a cold day, with intermittent sleet and rain showers. I was wet through to the skin. It was blowing a gale, too, when I set off for home in my invalid carriage. What's more, the wind was increasing in velocity, so by the time I'd half-reached my destination, the roads were awash, and my invalid carriage was being drenched with spray from any vehicle that passed me on the road. It was because of this that I came off the motorway, and took what I thought would be a safer route along one of the by-roads, I was wrong. For no sooner had I left the motorway, when my invalid carriage was struck by a gust of wind. I was hurtled along a country lane, out of control, until I collided with an oncoming car. The result of the accident was that I was conveyed by ambulance to the Medway Hospital, placed on a trolley, then stripped of my clothes. It was some time before I was seen by a young chap in a white coat. When he came he never asked me what had happened, if I was in pain, nothing. He just prodded me about with his index finger, then pronounced, 'There's no apparent injury', and told the nurses to get me dressed, which they did.

Once I'd been dressed, I was put into a wheel chair and taken to outpatients. My wife, who worked in hospital records, was called and told she could take me home. With the aid of two ambulance men, I was wheeled out to my wife's car, but after a struggle to get me in the passenger seat, the ambulance men gave up, and my wife went back into the hospital and brought the casualty reception sister to see me.

After a quick inspection by the casualty sister, I was taken back into casualty, where the hospital's registrar, a Mr Haq, came to examine me. X-rays were ordered, and in consequence it was discovered I had the following injuries:

fracture of the left fibular, fracture of the ninth rib, internal bleeding, pronounced external bruising.

These injuries did not include the extra pain that came from old dock injuries, such as spondylitis of the vertebra, osteoarthritis of the joints, and sacrococcygeal in my pelvis and left knee that was some of the consequences of previous accidents. I was, however, hospitalised for five days. When I asked Mr Haq if I could go home because I'd had enough of being in hospital. He was reluctant to allow this after seeing me walk with one permanently stiff leg from my wartime accident, and the other leg wrapped in plaster of Paris. I was however discharged and given an appointment to return in eight weeks' time to see a Mr Fleetcroft; but Mr Fleetcroft wasn't available. So instead I was to be seen by a deputy standing in for him.

The deputy, when I finally got to see him asked me, 'What have you come here for?'

I was dumbfounded by this man's attitude towards me, and the ignorance he showed of my case. After all, he had my medical record and x-ray photographs on his desk in front of him.

'If you'd looked at the medical notes and x-rays,' I told him, 'they may have enlightened you,' and I walked out of his surgery.

To me, nothing had changed in the way National Health Service patients were treated since my encounter with the staff at Orsett and St Barts hospitals, thirty years before, when I'd been injured on the RMS Orion in Tilbury Docks.

Due to this accident, I was off work for seven weeks. I know that I should have asked to be transferred to the Industrial Orthopaedic Society's Manor House Hospital, where I would have had my injuries properly treated. But I was too unwell at the time to even contemplate such a request.

Unfortunately, for reasons unbeknown to me, the Manor House Hospital was closed down some years ago. So it is with the greatest regret that I, like all of my National Insurance stamp and tax-paying countrymen, who are continually advised by political propagandists we have a "free health service", are at the mercy of a medical profession which, in my personal experience, would do well to be subjected as patients, to the sort of medical treatment they hand out to some of their National Health Service patients.

However, looking on the bright side from the point of view of a number of medical practitioners, the NHS should read NWS, that is the National Wealth Service, for it provides a forum whereby vulnerable patients are given the opportunity in many cases, to go private to jump a queue or join a long queue awaiting treatment. If one should be in a life threatening situation, one has little choice but to go private, pay up, as jumping the queue is possibly the only way of avoiding the consequences.

I have to say the system for treating some patients that is allowed to operate within the NHS these days, is conspicuously very similar to that which some back street shop keepers used in their business dealings during the 1939-45 war. That is, if you can get a queue to form, you can charge the customers almost any price within limits for your services, outside of the accepted legal regime. There is no doubt at all, the medical profession does hold our lives in their hands, all of us. From research, I recently discovered that over three hundred British soldiers, many suffering from "shell shock" or having been blinded from the effects of enemy gas attacks, were shot for cowardice during the 1914-18 war. Each soldier that was executed, so I understand, was required to be medically certified as being fit for his execution. Unfortunately, in my humble experience, I think the same doctors who signed those death warrants, were the same quacks that treated me in the NHS after my accidents; or maybe it was their contemporaries. Well! I'm sure that's not too far away from the truth of it, at least in *my* unfortunate experience. What do you think?

N.B. After I had written this account of my post-injury experiences under the NHS, I sent a copy to Bob Marshall-Andrews, my constituency MP. Within a week the British government rescinded all the "shot for cowardice" decisions made by non-line officers, and "fit for execution" certificates signed by doctors. If this account of my treatment under the NHS had anything to do with that decision—I would feel extremely pleased with my contribution to the exoneration of those soldiers' so-called "cowardice in the face of the enemy."

ADDENDUM 1

When, after I returned to work in the docks as a category 'C' man (light labour duties only), I was not able to go back to crane driving because I was unable to climb the three perpendicular flights of steel ladders, up to the crane platforms. So I was given the job of tea-boy with the ship's storing gang who I was working with when I was injured. In the mean time Dan, our dock's welfare officer, had talked me into applying for a place to study personnel management at the London School of Economics and Political Science. He had achieved this by the simple process of asking me what I thought of the then present system of employment in the docks, and when I told him I hadn't realised how corrupt it was, he simply said, 'Why don't you do something about it then?'

'What can I do about it?' I'd asked him.

'Write a proper employment plan for the docking industry,' he'd said.

'How do I do that?' I'd asked him, 'I'm semi-literate. I had very little schooling during the war, and what schooling I had was always spent in the lower forms.'

'Well, of course, you'll have to go to university; use your natural intelligence,' he said it in that matter of fact way of his.

'But I've got no qualifications,' I'd argued as an excuse, 'none of those CSE qualifications.'

'You don't have to bother about that,' he'd replied, 'you can apply as a mature student. Of course you'll have to go to night school and get some education before you go to sit the London School of Economics and Political Science entrance examinations. You'll need to start with English language. You'll have an Adult Education Centre where you live. Go and have a word with whoever is in charge.'

It was on a January evening that I made my way to the Adult Training Centre in Chatham, New Road, Kent. I was standing outside the building reading the various courses on the notice board, when a bloke in a jersey walked up behind me and said, 'Can I be of any help?'

'Well,' I'd replied, 'I need to study English language, but I'm semi-literate and don't know where to start.'

'Follow me,' he said, 'I'll show you where to go.'

I followed him to an office where a secretary was pumping away at a typewriter. You can imagine my surprise when she said, 'Oh, sir,' as we entered the room, 'there's a message here for you,' and she passed him a piece of paper.

He read the message then said to me, 'Come into my office.' Then he introduced himself, 'My name is Allen, I'm the principal of this Adult Education Centre. Now what can I do to help you?'

'I explained to him about Dan's expectations, about my lack of education, and about my semi-literacy, and that Dan had told me to start my education by attending night school to study English language. I also explained my reluctance to go into a class because I didn't want to be made a fool of as had always been the case when I was a school boy.'

Mr J. B. Allen, for that's who he was, just said 'Then I shall simply have to teach you myself.'

I spent one night a week for three weeks being taught the rudimentary principles as they relate to the English language by Mr Allen. Then, on the fourth week when I arrived for my lesson, he told me, 'You are advanced enough to go into a class with the other students,' and promptly led me into the English language class where he introduced me to a Mr Stern, the class teacher, who nursed me through the course until, at the end of term, he told me I was ready to sit for a CSE if I wished to—I told Dan.

'Right,' Dan said, 'you haven't got time for that. Now for the next phase, you have got to go to night school at your local college, and sign in for the personnel management course. You need to study industrial psychology, industrial law, and the rudimentary principles of the personnel management function. By the way, I've received a letter from LSE in reply to your request for a place. They've asked for a reference. I've sent in my recommendation. We shall have to wait and see if they are prepared to accept you. In the mean time, get on with your studies.'

When I went to enrol at West Kent College for the personnel management course, it was for the autumn term of 1962. The teacher for the course was a Mr Cummings, a supercilious, and I would add in my opinion a conceited, arrogant individual (you will see the reason for this description later). He asked me if I had any qualifications, and where I worked. When I told him I worked in the docklands of The Port of London, I had no qualifications, and I was signing in as a mature student, he told me that under the Institute of Personnel Management rules that was not possible, and that I required three O level passes as a minimum to qualify. But after I had told him he had better consult the IPM rule book, he changed his mind. Then, after I had paid my subscription, he gave me the appropriate diary of dates when I should attend the night classes, but he made it plain that he considered me, a common dock labourer, to be an unwanted impairment in his class of up and coming aspirants in the personnel management field of management expertise.

However, when I began my induction in the field of management studies, the lecturer in industrial law, a Welshman by the name of Mr Wardle, a tiny man who was no more than five feet six inches tall (168 cm) and as slim as a bean stick—he was just the opposite of Mr Cummings who was about five feet ten tall (178 cm), obese, with fat flabby cheeks, and who had a habit of continually using a wooden pick on his teeth during lessons. Not only did I take to studying industrial law, but this was also because Mr Wardle was a brilliant teacher. In fact, when I went up to LSE, the law notes I made when Mr Wardle was teaching, stood me in good stead when studying under that eminent lecturer in industrial law, Professor Khan Freud.

Then, on the final night class in personnel management studies at West Kent College, in June 1963, Mr Wardle asked me if Cummings had registered me to sit the IPM external examinations. When I told him he had not, he advised me to challenge him and ask him why. As Cummings' class followed Mr Wardle's, I waited until the other class students had finished their kowtowing and good-byes. Then I challenged him as to why he had not entered me for the IPM examinations. He puckered his nose, used his tooth pick on his teeth, and in that supercilious, sniggering, cocky way he had when he spoke to me said, 'Ask my secretary and make an appointment to see me in my office.' He then flicked a finger at me, turned his back, and walked off.

Fortunately, as I was the tea boy to a ship's stores gang, I was able to get away for an appointment with Cummings on the following week. When I knocked on his office door at the appointed time he ordered, 'Wait.' Then after about five minutes he ordered, 'Come.' When I entered his office he was sitting at his desk in a high chair, with his back to an open window, flicking through a file of papers on his desk that I can only assume related to my attendance and academic record while attending night class at The West Kent College. He left me standing while he asked me, 'Now what is it you wanted to see me about?' As if he hadn't known.

'Why you failed to advise me about the IPM examination date and refused to enter me for the examinations.'

'I told you,' he said, 'that you were not academically qualified to take the examinations.'

'So you did,' I replied, 'and I told you I was a mature student and didn't need academic qualifications.'

'Well,' he said with a smirk on his face, and a convulsive laugh that caused his double chin to ripple like a jelly, 'it's too late now for you to be entered for this year's examinations.'

'You could have told me that last week,' I said, 'instead of dragging me all the way over here from Tilbury docks. But it doesn't matter,' I continued, 'because I have applied to sit the Personnel Management Diploma Course at The London School of Economics and Political Science.'

'You have what?' he blurted out. 'You? You? You've had the temerity to apply to the LSE for a place? Do you know that over six hundred graduate students apply for a place each year to study for a Diploma in Personnel Management?'

'Yes,' I said, 'I was told that.'

'And you,' he sniggered, 'a dock labourer with no academic qualifications have had the temerity to apply to LSE for a place on one of the most revered academic diplomas courses in management?' Then burst out laughing.

I waited until he had mopped the tears from his bloodshot eyes before I told him: 'The LSE criteria doesn't only base student entry on academic qualification alone, would-be students have to attend a viva to test for knowledge; and intelligence is at the forefront of LSE selection procedures.'

Cummings burst out laughing again before saying: 'So you think you may be selected on your intelligence? That's if you can get invited to an interview. Ha-ha-ha!'

'Oh! I've been interviewed, Mr Cummings,' I told him, 'and I've sat the examinations and attended a viva. In fact, I've been given leave of absence by the London Dock Labour Board to attend the one-year Diploma course in Personnel Management at the LSE. I register as a mature student and begin my studies in the Michaelmas term that begins on 4th October (1963).'

Cummings sat in his chair shaking like a leaf, his fat jowls rippling like an incoming tide across his face. He had gone a sort of battleship-grey colour, and began leaning precariously back towards the window. I thought he was having a heart attack; but I had no sympathy for him. He was to me nothing more than a pompous, snobbish, tooth-picking slob. I just walked out of his office hoping thankfully never to meet the likes of him again—and thank God the Almighty, in the academic world I joined at LSE, I never did.

ADDENDUM 2

My induction into the world of higher education wasn't to be as traumatic as I thought it might be. Dan Foley, the Tilbury Docks Welfare Office and my mentor (or was it tormentor?), had assured me that I would soon feel my feet, so to speak. 'Remember,' he'd said, 'most of the other students on the course will never have been in any form of employment. They will know how to read and write "proper", he'd said with a smile. But you *do* know about working in industry, and you've got the scars to prove it.' How right he was.

As I stood in the queue to register, I began talking to a chap by the name of Paul Smith. Paul was about the same age as myself (I was thirty three at the time). He had a degree in some subject either from Oxford or Cambridge, but had spent several years in the RAF before going out to Rhodesia to work in the mining industry. He had been given leave of absence to come to LSE to study for a Post Graduate Diploma in Personnel Management by his employer. Of course, we had nothing in common, which is possibly why we got on so well together. After registration, and other formalities that students have to go through, we made our way to what was to be our study room. Our Industrial Psychology lecturer and tutor, was a Mr Holms who called the class to order. Then he said, 'Right. Now I want each one of you to introduce yourself to the class beginning with,' and he pointed to the student sitting next to him on his left. I cannot remember who it was who begun the introductions, but I've never forgotten the way the introductions preceded. It went something like this, 'My name is X and I've come down from Oxford. I'm a graduate in [subject]'.

Then, 'I'm Y and I've come over from Dublin. I'm a graduate in [subject]'

I was sitting at the end of the table, when it came to my turn. Mr Holms said, 'And you are?'

You cannot possibly know how I felt, I had nothing to offer in the way of academic education, so I simply said, 'I'm Henry T. Bradford. I'm one degree under. I'm a docker from Tilbury docks.'

Mr Holms, I have to point out, had a caste in one of his eyes. So it was fortunate one really did not know who he was looking at. Then he said, 'Do you mean you have come here straight out of the docks?'

'No, sir,' I replied, 'I came here off the quay.'

What amazed me was that although most of the students turned and smiled at me; no one laughed. I got on like a house on fire with Mr Holms, as I did with all the academic staff—especially Keith Thurley who, along with Mr Holms, were my course tutors—and Nancy Seear who was head of department until she was elevated to the House of Lords with the title of Baroness Seear.

During my time at LSE, the only educational establishment where I ever felt at home among intelligent, highly educated mortals of so many academic disciplines, I met a fellow student who was to have a profound effect on the way I looked on my capabilities and myself in the future. All the time I'd spent at school (except for one brief period when I was at junior school), form teachers had always down-marked mine and my contemporary classmates' work. It seemed to me our teachers were under orders to denigrate everything we did, until we lost confidence in ourselves. Everyone did so in those days; before and during the war when I attended school, whatever any one of us said or wrote was wrong. Of course, this continual "put you down" policy had a profound effect on our confidence, but when I arrive at LSE I discovered that, except for the posh accents, my intellectual reasoning powers were equal to any one of my fellow students.

After a period of lectures, written essays and tutorials, I was put in a group of four to carry out research into the training scheme of a major civil engineering company. The chosen leader for our group was John Deeks, a Cambridge graduate, a real egghead if there ever was one. He spearheaded our group into producing possibly the best researched programmes by students on the Diploma in Personnel Management course at LSE at that time. It was an exercise from which I learnt how to separate facts from fiction; how to construct concurrent events into logical sequence and follow up with a report that was readable and understandable to those with even a smattering of knowledge of the subject. In other words, it gave me the ability and knowledge I required to carry out Dan's plan (Dan, my own personal Spengali), for a change in the permanent employment status of registered dockworkers throughout the United Kingdom, but more especially the Port of London.

At the end of my course at LSE, Dan obtained a further six months leave of absence for me from the LDLB, in which time I was to write my report and employment plan that I called "A Docker's Plan for the Port Transport Industry". I named it "a docker's plan" to show that if a docker could write such a plan, then surely it should not be beyond the capability of the Port Authority Executives or the port employers' managers to have done something in a similar vein?

However, on completing my plan and returning to the dock, Dan kept a copy then suggested that I should send copies to those people who were in a position to change things. Therefore copies were sent to: Mr Albert Murray, MP. for Gravesend, Kent; Mr Dudley Perkins, the Director General of the Port of London Authority, at Trinity Square, London (he wrote to ask me for a further copy as the one I sent him had vanished); Miss Nancy Seear, and my course tutor Mr Keith Thurley at LSE (unfortunately Mr Thurley was on sabbatical in Japan at that time); the editor of the Daily Mirror, who returned his copy—the Daily Mirror failed to print any part of the document; Mr Jack Harper of Maltbys, Mr Edwards of Scruttons, and Captain Magnus Work of West African Terminals—all three in charge of stevedoring contracting companies, and the General Secretary of the Transport and General Workers Union, and

Jack Dash, Chairman of the London Dockworkers Liaison Committee.

I have no doubt that Dan distributed a few copies, because sections of the plan that the labours contractors could use without resorting to undermine the Dock Workers (Regulation of Employment) Act, were put into operation by them.

It was, however, several years after my employment plan had been written, and disseminated to those persons listed above, that Lord Devlin came on the scene and phase (i) and (ii) of The Devlin Report (a report not dissimilar to mine) was published and introduced in the docks. Unfortunately, the new employment scheme came too late to benefit the men it was meant for. Containerisation had arrived and with it the methodical closure of the upper docks that brought about the demise of the greatest port complex in the world.

Yes. The upper docks of the great Port of London were gone forever, and so too were the men that had worked within its complex system of stevedoring, ship repair and ship refurbishing operations, lock gate keepers, tug boat crews, "Smoky Joe's" cafés, and the many other subsidiary occupations that had made it the greatest conurbation of dock facilities developed on this earth. The east end of London shall never be the same again.

Amen.

A Docker's Plan for the Port Transport Industry

Preface

In the twelve years since I first became a registered port worker, the dominant impression left on my mind has been of the total disregard of the port employers, and of the National Dock Labour *Board,* for the dignity of those men employed in the Port Transport Industry. Little, if any, attention has been paid to the human problems of the port transport industry since the endeavours of Ernest Bevin in the late and early nineteenth century. Over the last few years, mainly through the threat of unofficial action, wage increases have been won: but other needs, e.g. welfare, safety, training, the placement of injured or permanently sick men returning to the industry, these have been almost totally disregarded. If what follows helps in alleviating one fraction of the inhumanity of the present port transport system of employment, then the time taken up by writing this paper shall have been well spent.

Introduction

The "Dock Workers (Regulation of Employment) Act" setting out directions for change in the port transport industry, was introduced in 1947. Since that time very few of the suggested innovations have been carried into effect.

This does not mean that some dictates of the "regulations" have not been put into operation; some necessary schemes have been introduced, but on a very limited scale, e.g. with regard to training and some meagre welfare facilities; but the present arrangements are totally inadequate as they relate to the necessary skill requirements of a major industry, such as the British port transport industry.

The scheme now in operation covers neither the needs of the men for "adequate welfare and other ancillary employee services" nor of the employers for "the correct and economic use of the registered dock labour force".

Unfortunately, the pressure for innovation and change that the Dock Labour Act was undoubtedly meant to create within the industry, has in no way been utilised.

This paper has been written, therefore, with the direct intention of showing, from a docker's point of view, the major weaknesses in the present Dock Labour Scheme, and the need for a complete registered dock worker control employment scheme within the port transport industry. In writing this "plan" I have tried not to allow my own personal bias (which quite naturally favours the dock workers) to obscure the logic and economic reasoning behind my argument. Many men, according to their position within the port transport industry, will see the contents of this paper from different perspectives to my own: some will agree with what is written, and some may be offended; but, whatever may be said about the plan outlined here, my only hope is that the outcome will be to the benefit of, and not to the detriment of port registered dock workers, and the port transport industry in general.

To some people in other industries this plan may appear primitive, but the fact that other industries may have had advanced schemes in operation for decades is of little consolation to port transport workers in whose industry such a plan, if effected, would be little short of an industrial personnel revolution; therefore:

(i) The Need for a Comprehensive Employment Plan for Registered Dockworkers

The most important point to remember when dealing with the application of labour in any industry, is that all labour must be applied in such a way that the best possible results are obtained from its deployment. This is not only good business; it is economic necessity. To waste any form of manpower, skilled or unskilled, is not only a social crime, it is economic suicide in a land such as ours whose most valuable natural resource is the muscle and inventive brainpower of its people, the general living standard can only be maintained or raised by the united effort of us all.

In the port transport industry at present manpower wastage is a prime cause of unrest. Under the existing dock labour scheme there is no possible way of solving this problem or of extending, with much chance of success, welfare and other necessary ancillary employee benefits. What the industry needs is a completely new Labour Administration Scheme. The plan that is set out in these pages, however imperfect it may be, is an attempt to construct a scheme that would not only benefit the workers in the industry, but also alleviate the human and material wastage associated with the present working conditions in the docks.

(ii) The Framework of the Plan

(1) The present framework of the National Dock Labour Board should be incorporated into a National Ports Authority which would be divided into sectors similar to those of the present Port Authorities—e.g. The major ports, for example, London, Liverpool, Southampton, Rochester, Hull, etc.

(2) The present Port Authorities should be totally nationalised and controlled by the proposed National Ports Authority or, alternatively, the present Port Authorities should themselves set up a National Ports Authority into which the National Dock Labour Board would be integrated.

(3) All Port Registered Workers should come under the jurisdiction of the new Port Labour Authorities operating within the framework of the proposed National Ports Authority as set out above.

(4) All Port Registered Workers should be paid a "guaranteed weekly wage".

(iii) Benefits of the Plan

Several benefits could be derived from this revised scheme of working.

(1) Recruitment under a National Ports Authority, as well as taking into account the various factors affecting labour turnover, could be geared in each port to the shipping expected at any given time.

(2) Men drawing a guaranteed weekly wage as permanent labour could, by a direct system of control, be deployed with greater efficiency.

(3) The men, by identifying themselves with a specific employer—the Port Labour Authority—and freed

from the present frustration of their work and wage insecurity, would take a greater interest in the running of their dock.

(4) From the increased sense of responsibility amongst the men it would be possible to set up Dockworker Committees to deal with problems arising from internal grievances, e.g. amenities (washing facilities), canteens, and malpractices etc. which could be dealt with. These committees would only be effective if the parent port employers were able to put into practice any agreements reached.

(5) Imperative innovations could be introduced, e.g.

    (a) Training programmes for every skilled job, i.e. crane drivers/winch drivers, forklift trucks, etc.;

    (b) Tighter and more rigorously enforced safety measures; reduction of accidents by the removal of dangerous working practices;

    (c) Internal selection and promotion;

    (d) Sick and injury pay schemes;

    (e) Better retirement pensions;

    (f) Death benefits for dependants of men killed at work.

(6) The men would more readily accept changes in their normal work practice, e.g. the introduction of three shifts working on certain types of cargoes. The labour force would be given a much-needed flexibility in its deployment.

(iv) Application of the Plan

(1) The present system of the "free call" should be abolished. In its place, and with a Port Labour Authority controlling the deployment of all labour, contract work carried out on ship-board should be allocated on a "gang rota system". This gang rota system should be based on "gang preference", i.e. the men should retain their right to be allocated to the employer of their choice and should be able to register accordingly with the Port Labour Authority, only being allocated elsewhere if there is no "work call" from that particular employer. In this way there would be a rota within a rota and men registered for work with a specific employer would join a queue of preference, taking their turn on a rota for the work available and at the same time being available to the "call" of other employers.

To enable "employer gang preference allocation schemes to work" the following conditions would have to be met:

(a) Initially the men must be allowed to form themselves into gangs;

(b) There should be machinery to enable men to withdraw from a gang if they so desire, and;

(c) There should be machinery to enable a majority of the gang to request the removal of one or more of their number.

This "employer preference—gang allocation scheme" is based on recognition of the following facts:

(a) Men work better as informal "self-selecting" groups;

(b) Most men prefer to work for a particular employer or ship worker;

(c) Employers and ship workers prefer to employ the same men;

(d) Most men generally choose to work for a particular firm, either because they know the ship worker, or because they prefer to handle certain types of cargo. By knowing and being known by the ship worker the men act more responsibly in their employment, and by working on one particular kind of cargo, they become more efficient in its handling; the benefits to the employer are obvious.

(2) All quay-work and ship quay discharging, ship quay loading, ship discharged cargoes delivery (imports), ship cargo striking (exports)—should be carried out by the Port Labour Authority's quay gangs. The Port Labour Authority should also be responsible for:

(a) Training mechanical appliance operators;

(b) Supplying and maintaining those appliances;

(c) Internal recruitment of persons suitable for training as operators for those appliances.

This would ensure that both operators and appliances would be fully utilised, and that mechanical aids could be more easily transferred within each dock according to the particular needs of different jobs. In addition appliance operators could be charged "pro-rata" to a gang during the period for which the appliance is required, thereby allowing for its release as soon as it is needed elsewhere.

(3) Contracting firms should continue to be responsible for the discharging of ships cargoes. This would include over-side, other than quay landing, craft delivery barge, and Captains Entry and accommodation craft discharge, but would not include such "craft" to be loaded direct from the quay.

(4) The present system of engagement should be carried on; men should continue to be engaged on a particular contract "continuity to a hold". The method of "gang transfer" advocated by the employers and trade unions would not be necessary because the Port Labour Authority would be able to strengthen any particular labour force on request from an employer.

(5) It must be accepted by men drawing a weekly wage that, after the "a.m." call, they should be prepared to split into two SD the "p.m." for the afternoon period. With such a system in operation the proposed weekly wage would, on the commencement of a piecework operation, have to be broken down into an hourly rate. The day work rate would take the form of a guaranteed minimum: thus, as under the present operational arrangements, if piecework earnings fell below the hourly rate then the hourly rate would be paid.

(6) With the abolition of the "free call" system; "C" men would also come under the direct control of the Port Labour Authority who would be responsible for finding them suitable employment within the industry. The benefits that would accrue from such an arrangement is that "C" category men:

(a) Should be called on to work eleven turns each week;

(b) They should be paid the same basic weekly wage as "A" category men;

(c) And this would prevent the use of "C" men as a form of cheap labour; i.e. three days "fall-back pay" for six or more reporting turns each week;

(d) It would prevent "C" men having to apply to the National Assistance Board when on a fall-back week.

(e) It would induce the persons responsible for the employment of "C" men to train them in the operation and use of mechanical aids, or in other jobs which would reduce the pressure on the "A" men in the labour force and thereby spread the work load more evenly;

(f) Light labour jobs such as coopers, needle-men, and shed needys (needys being men employed as handy men) could be filled by "C" men and not, as at present, by "A" men who are "keeping out of the way for a day" in order to be picked up for more remunerative jobs;

(g) The retention of "C" men in the industry would help to retain future checkers; experienced men so necessary to the industries;

(h) "C" men would no longer be thrown onto the Ministry of Labour, which has great difficulty in finding them alternative employment.

(7) One of the fundamental problems of the Port Transport Industry is the inability of the employers to set up any system for the proper delegation of responsibility in the lower echelons of their

organisation. The *employers* would do well to remember the old saying: 'the British Army is run by its NCOs'. A much more comprehensive scheme of ganger selection is needed than the present one, whereby any Tom, Dick or Harry is asked to be a ganger's job by a ship worker. What is required is a permanent pool of trained down hold foremen and quay gangs to take charge of the allocated ship and quay working gangs.

(8) The pensioning off of the over 65s should retain a recall clause up to the age of 68 for skilled men such as crane-drivers, winch-drivers, clerks and checkers; such men should be eligible for recall for periods in times of skilled labour shortage, subject to two conditions being met:

    (a) That the man should agree to his recall;

    (b) That the doctor should pass the man fit for recall. In addition, those reaching the age of 65 should not be retired until after the holiday period is over—except for health reasons or at the man's own request.

(9) With all men being under the direct control of the Port Labour Authority, each man should be medically examined every eighteen months and medically graded accordingly.

(10) All men returning to work after either sickness or injury should automatically be placed on an "r" register for at least seven days; this would:

    (a) Prevent men "going sick" in order to avoid a job that they did not like or in order to save themselves for a job that they particularly wanted.

(b) Stop men weakened by illness or injury from going straight back onto jobs where they could receive further injury, and from being a physical burden on their fellows during their rehabilitation.

(11) Thought should be given to the introduction of two-shift working; this would free berths and thereby minimise the need for expanding the number of berths. The capital saved could be spent on new handling equipment, on the modernisation of the present sheds and quays, and on providing better amenities for port workers.

(12) Crane drivers should not be permitted to spend their whole working day at the controls of a crane. The reasons for this suggestion are both physiological and psychological:

(a) It is detrimental to a man's health to work for long periods in a confined space; it causes bad blood circulation and the constant concentration creates tension in the nerves and. strain on the eyes;

(b) It is detrimental for a man to be separated for long periods from his companions; strain and tension create frustration, this can create an apathetic attitude and thus increase the possibility of serious accidents.

(9) To overcome this difficulty all top hands should also be trained as crane drivers and should take their turn in tending the "hatch and crane". Such an arrangement would have several advantages:

(a) It would reduce the mental strain on crane drivers;

(b) It would encourage those men who cannot stand the long hours alone as crane drivers to reacquaint themselves with their old skills;

(c) It would create a more flexible labour force and thus help to increase output;

(d) The "mobile (tea break) period" would be automatically shortened; crane drivers would only have to travel one way for their tea break, compared with two at present, thereby saving time.

(v) Health & Safety

The appointment of full time safety officers is long overdue in the Port Transport Industry. The persons so appointed should be known as Port Health & Safety Officers, and their duties should cover the following:

(a) Working in close conjunction with the Factory Inspectorate and/or Board of Trade;

(b) Investigating all reports of faulty gear and tracing the sources of such gear; reporting his findings to the Traffic Officer or Superintendent responsible for the ship or quay from which the complaint came, to the manufacturers of the gear and to the suppliers, and to the Dock Health and Safety Committees; reactions, a.m. and p.m. The a.m. labour surplus would stand by for the morning labour supplement duty, and

(c) To make tours of inspection of the docks to ensure that safety standards are maintained and fully complied with;

(d) Completing accident reports for the Port Labour Authority and/or the contractor concerned, and submitting such reports to the appropriate authority. The accident report should contain all the relevant facts relating to the accident: e.g. the place where it occurred, the cause of the accident, i.e. whether it was due to carelessness, faulty equipment etc. and whether the accident was avoidable to The Health & Safety Committees, with a view to preventing, if possible, the recurrence of such an accident. The Health & Safety officer's report should be studied in detail. The committees should also debate whether the correct conclusions have been drawn as to the cause of the accident concerned.

    (e) Compiling accident statistics; isolating the major factors leading to accidents, and formulating plans to combat these factors.

    (f) Implementing a safety clothing drive—seeing that footwear, gloves and tough and durable working clothes are made available to the men, and even, perhaps, employing a hatter to design a "safety cloth cap"?

(7) Setting up Dock Safety Committees; the duties of these committees should include:

    (a) Discussing and applying ways and means of reducing the number of accidents;

    (b) Bringing to the notice of the port authorities infringements of safety regulations, and the occurrence of dangerous working practices;

    (c) Trying out and discussing the advantages and disadvantages of different types of protective clothing and its suitability for the industry;

(d) Bringing to the notice of port-registered dockworkers the findings of the committee and encouraging a general "safety conscience".

(8) Stopping any job that in the opinion of the port safety officer was dangerous or unsafe until such time as the work was made safe to the satisfaction of the safety officer. Any time so lost should be charged against the firm responsible for the operation that caused the stoppage. As a result of this authority being vested in the port safety officer, ship workers would ensure that safety regulations were fully complied with. In addition, any gang that considered it was being asked to carry out a dangerous practice, or use unsafe equipment, should appeal to The Health & Safety Officer for a decision regarding that work operation.

(9) Corresponding with importing and exporting firms and advising them of the best possible way to abolish dangerous packaging practices, e.g. the flat bands at present used for binding tea chests and other containers should be replaced by round wire bands that do not cut when they break.

(10) Advising contractors in the purchasing of new rope and wires—e .g. in the use of Swedish spliced steel ferrule wires in place of the aluminium non—spliced ferrule wires at present used by some contracting firms (the advantage of the steel ferruled wire being that it does not draw when under strain).

The object at all times must be to prevent accidents. An accident avoided is a unit of skilled manpower made available.

Protective Clothing: The present system of safety clothing being ordered by welfare officers should be abandoned as inadequate. Instead the sole distribution of protective clothing should be the responsibility of the port safety officers administered through Dock Clothing Shops. Up to now men ordering protective footwear have often had to wait for weeks before their order has been delivered; this is not good enough as all types of safety clothing should be available when required.

If the dock clothing shops are unable to cope with this work, then the Port Labour Authority should make itself responsible for setting up protective clothing shops of its own; such shops should contain every item of protective clothing required within the port transport industry.

The Port Labour Authority should continue the scheme of 'weekly repayments' for protective clothing at present run by the National Dock Labour Board.

(vi) Welfare Facilities

The welfare facilities within the port transport industry should be extended under the following headings:

(1) Pensions:

    (a) Arrangements should be made to increase pensions to a level of two-thirds the normal flat weekly wage;

    (b) Within a nationalised port transport industry; pension administration costs could be reduced by pensions being paid through Post Offices or banks.

(2) Sick Pay:

    (a) Contributory sick-pay schemes should be introduced; this scheme should be compulsory

227

and its terms should be written into the contracts of employment of all registered port transport workers.

(b) Sick-pay should be not less than two-thirds the normal flat weekly wage, less National Insurance or Industrial Injuries benefit.

(c) Men absent from work through sickness or injury should be eligible for benefit payment, the qualifying periods should be:

(1) Sickness benefit after two weeks absence;

(2) Industrial injury benefit after seven days absence;

(3) Compassionate Leave or other leave should continue under the present "pool excuse system"; i.e. on the recommendation of port managers;

(4) Sports and Social Clubs. The present independent sports and social clubs should be absorbed into the port labour authorities sports and social clubs; in this way their activities could be broadened to cater for the whole of the labour force, and thereby give different dock sections of the labour force the opportunity of meeting each other in sporting events;

(5) Canteen facilities. The present state of the majority of the catering establishments available to port transport workers is both disgusting and deplorable. The Tilbury docks canteen was built to house strike breakers during the 1912 dock strike. This is generally not the fault of the port catering managers, who do wonders with the equipment and buildings

that they are provided with, but these facilities are totally inadequate. This is an area in which immediate and drastic action is called for.

(6) First Aid Training is of significant importance in the port transport industry and this fact should be rammed home to the port workers. A port transport-training scheme in first aid should be instituted and run in close cooperation with the medical centres under the control of the port doctor. The Port Labour Authority should aim at having two trained first aides at each shed when work is in progress. Persons in the gangs who have qualified as first aides should be paid an annual supplement or bonus.

(7) Medical Centres. The present Port Medical Services should be integrated with medical centres run by the Port Labour Authority. The system now in use whereby the port authorities and the National Dock Labour Board run separate medical establishments is a costly duplication of effort.

One method of distributing the cost of medical services more evenly amongst the various authorities would be to run medical centres on a basis similar to that on the Slough Industrial Estate: thus any person working for the port authorities, the port contractors, the ship-repair or dock maintenance contractors or other port services would be eligible for treatment at the medical centre; the cost of the centre would be met by a levy on employers made on a per capita basis or according to the time spent in treatment or on any other agreeable basis. It is to be hoped that by contributing towards such a service the employers would become more safety conscious.

(8) Welfare Officers: Each dock should have a fully trained and competent welfare officer. The duties of the welfare officer should be extended to cover all the areas of welfare outlined in (1) to (7) above.

(vii) Training

The Need for Comprehensive Training:

A training programme has been set up to train new entrants to the port transport industry: this programme also covers, to a certain extent, the training of told hands—for example, in the use of mechanical handing appliances. However the scheme only goes a very short way towards fulfilling the training needs of the skilled manpower in the industry. The laissez-faire attitude of the present National Dock Labour Board towards training is partly to blame for the development of this situation. What is now required in this field is a completely new outlook and approach to the training problems of the industry. Not only should the training of recruits be covered, but a comprehensive training plan should be drawn up to ensure that no man can hold a position of responsibility in the industry until he has acquired, through training, the necessary skill and knowledge for the job. Such a training plan should be the responsibility of the Port Labour Authority.

The Selection of Personnel to be trained:

The selection of the right persons for training for responsible positions is a necessary prerequisite of any effective training policy. Particular attention must be paid in an industry like the port transport industry to the relationship between the man in the supervisory position and the group that he is leading. Every care must be taken to ensure that the group leader is fully aware of the norms of the group under his control and of what they as a group are attempting to achieve. This means that the natural group leader will, in many cases, be the best candidate for training for responsibility or, alternatively, a formally trained ganger or foreman must be injected into a particular group on the basis of his understanding of that group's needs and objectives. It is to be hoped that in this way the general good of the industry will be matched to the general good of the men themselves. In every case, the persons selected for training must be, without exception, capable of setting a high standard of performance and of putting into practice the knowledge gained from the training programmes.

The Objectives of Training:

The training policy of the port transport industry should aim at:

(1) Making working conditions safer by ensuring better methods of work;
(2) Less damaged work and less careless faulty work;
(3) Higher production through greater efficiency;
(4) Teaching every man to appreciate the advantages of mechanical work aids and to utilise them correctly;
(5) Ensuring that every man knows the basis for his actions, and that he earns his wages. This does not mean that the port workers should continue to subsidise the general public by their vast output at ludicrously low piecework rates.

Induction Training:

Induction training programmes should cover the elementary requirements of the industry; e.g.:

(1) How to lay a rope, i.e. bottom bite or top bite;

(2) How to move heavy casework without danger;

(3) The best way to work into a cargo, i.e. discharging;

(4) The correct way to make a safe set, loading or discharging.

The Training of Down-Hold Foremen:

Down-hold foremen should be trained in the art of loading and discharging the cargo; e.g.:

(1) How to stow (loading) and break out cargoes (discharging);

(2) How to utilise the mechanical aids available, if any;

(3) How to use the present equipment; i.e. bull-winch wires, cleats and heel blocks;

(4) The correct way to stow delicate and precious cargoes. All importers should be asked to help in formulating handbooks showing the best way to handle and stow their particular product;

(5) How to utilise every inch of ship stowage space.

The Training of Quay-Foremen:

Quay-gang foremen should be trained in sorting and shed stowing "C" cargoes and of imports and exports; they must work with other quay-gang foremen under the direction of a mobile labour foreman. The following suggestions are made for improvements in present practice:

(1) With regard to imports, a plan of intended shed stowage should be made prior to delivery; imports could be then sorted in such a way as to allow direct lines of delivery; this would also prevent delivery gangs from working at cross purposes;

(2) Exports should be sorted according to the nature of the goods; dirty goods for numbers one and five

232

hatches could then be placed in the vicinity of those hatches instead of the present practice of putting them anywhere that might suit the striking gang's fancy;

(3) Mobile foremen should have prior knowledge of the ship and her cargo; the gangers working under a foreman and preparing to receive goods for or from a ship would then have the necessary knowledge and encouragement to work the cargo in such a way that would benefit them as a team, rather than as separate bodies.

(4) A positive way of ensuring that exports are properly received and shed stowed, would be to give the striking gangs continuity with the ship's gangs after their receiving operation.

Training in all these matters is imperative.

Merit Money for Trained Personnel:

Apart from the induction training, all other skilled training satisfactorily completed and examinations passed should be merit rated; this rate would be paid in the form of a weekly bonus or supplement on top of the basic rate and **would** be a permanent payment to those who have satisfactorily completed a course of training. Two points concerning this merit money should be borne in mind:

(1) Men passing the examinations and receiving the increase must understand that they are still eligible to work as members of a gang;

(2) It would be advisable only to put newly merit-rated men into working gangs; older men might resent such. As for the training of Crane Drivers, Winch

233

Drivers and Hatchway men, these three jobs are closely aligned and call for closely related skills, e.g.:

1. Cranes are temperamental appliances and a crane driver must be capable of driving many different types of crane, each one having special characteristics of its own.

2. The person chosen to tend a hatch needs to have an intimate knowledge of the appliance that he indirectly controls; the same conditions apply to the relationship between the hatchway men and the winch-drivers.

3. Because of this close tie-up between these three jobs it is suggested that:

(1) No man should be allowed to operate a ship's crane until he has had a 'reasonable period' of ship working and ship-side experience.

(2) No man should be allowed to become a crane driver until he has completed at least two years as a down holder; this will ensure that every crane driver knows the reason for the orders he is given, and the operations he is required to carry out.

4. NIB. A system of work training for these three categories of workers should be under the auspices of the Port Labour Authority, and cover not only the training of winch and crane drivers but also induction training in cargo handling. Such induction training should be carried out on cargoes known to be day-work operations. In this way persons being trained as crane and winch drivers could learn to operate their respective machines at a safe and comfortable pace without being subject to the pressures of piece-working and of men who are on piece-rates. This training scheme would thus cover not only the operator training of crane and winch drivers but would also:

(a) Give the necessary cargo handling experience to new recruits;

(b) Help to offset the costs of training by productive work and by a method of working which would increase productivity;

(c) Give all those being trained for such jobs the essential practical experience for which there is no substitute.

5. For the training of winch-drivers, the setting up of quay-side winches should be installed. These could be used for:

(a) The training of winch-drivers in ship work and quay operations;

(b) The "yard striking" of freight, as opposed to "bank striking" of heavy export cargoes, and "yard delivery" as opposed to "bank delivery" of heavy imported cargoes, and for topping out purposes. The derricks could be of any lifting capacity.

(c) The training of future deck hands in the correct use of "guys" and "lazy guys" and in the meaning of the hand signals used on the quay, on and off the ship.

The Training of 'C' Men

The training of 'C' men to do jobs which are within their physical capabilities is an immediate necessity. There are many jobs that can be filled by unskilled men who have no training, i.e. needle men, and needys—but "C" men find even these jobs difficult to obtain under the present system. There should be a job reservation scheme for category 'C' labour and such unskilled jobs as needle men etc. should be reserved for light labour men. Their jobs do require some training the port doctor should be consulted as to the suitability of "C" men for the work ii question.

"C" men could also be trained as mechanical appliance operators e.g. stacker-trucks, mobile cranes, electric quay trucks. In this way not only would unskilled "C" labour be turned into skilled operatives but the whole of the industry's manpower force would be more productive and more flexible.

The Training of "C" Men checkers:

The present scheme, which allows "C" men checkers to be allocated to supplement the OST clerks, should be revised. It is not the place of "C" men in the port transport industry to act as lackeys or play second fiddle to tally clerks; they work in the industry for their livelihood, not as supplements to the Clerks' Register. There are several ways in which this problem of using "C" men as cheap labour could be overcome; for example, "C" men checkers could be allocated to an OST on certain jobs, e.g. ship-loading, meat pool, etc. But before this could be done they would have to receive some formal training; it is obvious that men who have been doing manual work for many years, probably most of their lives, will need some form of training before they can confidently switch to carrying out clerical duties. It is suggested, therefore, that:

  (a) Men injured at work or suffering from a permanent illness or disability should be advised, prior to their return to work, whether or not they should request to be placed on the Checker Register;

(b) Those men who do wish to be placed on the Checker Register should be given a short period of clerical training;

(c) When the Clerical Register needs to be brought up to strength, short-listed "C" men who have been on the Checker Register for some time should be allowed to apply for transfer to the Clerical Register; or, alternatively, employers should be asked to recommend "C" men checkers for transfer to full clerical duties on the basis of their knowledge and assessment of a man's likely ability in a full clerical capacity;

(d) Men selected to become clerks from a category "C" docker-checker list, should be made and paid up to OST clerks. This would mean they would only be eligible for such duties as quay delivery, striking, meat pool, etc. *after* they had served a probationary period on this kind of work, and had passed the clerical examination, only then they should be given full clerical status.

Notes:

(1) It is probably advisable to concentrate on winter training schedules for most forms of advanced port work training, i.e. as crane drivers, winch drivers, down-hold foremen etc. Generally speaking, after the holiday period is over, more labour is available in the port transport industry and winter training programmes would help to offset the unequal distribution of the labour force at this time;

(2) Standards of performance and minimum qualifications for entry should be set up for each job; for example, employers should not be permitted to promote a man to the position of ship worker or quay labour foreman unless or until he has the necessary qualifications—i.e. has been passed as proficient in every branch of port working; only in this way will respect be brought to positions like those of ship worker and quay foreman thereby giving the men of the industry something to strive for and achieve.

(viii) Wages

(1) The present system of employer and trade union negotiation of basic wage rates should continue, within the framework of a National Incomes Policy. But as far as local rates are concerned, "dock rate boards" should be set up to deal with problems and disputes arising from loose or tight piecework rates. Disputes over piecework rates generally occur on shipboard and the chief causes of dissension are:

(a) Rates for long distance working—i.e. in cupboards and alleyways;

(b) Rates for awkward working, i.e. in 'tween deck cupboards and deep tanks; where there is a lack of adequate headroom and where obstacles arise from double-banking, i.e. two gangs working in the same hold;

(c) Rates for bad cargo stowage: e.g. birdcage bag work stowage, cut timber over-stowed on logs, heavy and light logs stowed together and calling for a continuous change of purchase.

238

At the present time the piecework rate of all jobs remains unchanged until an "area committee" has been called to review and re-assess the job under dispute; and since such committees are generally composed entirely of employer representatives, its findings are felt to be biased against the port worker. The proposed local dock rate board should be made up of both employers' and workers' representatives; they should attempt to reach agreement on local rates for all disputed work. These agreements should be standardised so that ships returning to the local dock will not immediately open the same disputes as were settled on their last visit. Any awards made by the local dock rate board would be subject to increases on a pro-rata basis in line with any nationally negotiated wage increases. It is to be expected that at the outset the proposed dock rate boards would be called into numerous disputes and would have to be in session constantly, but that after this initial phase, lasting perhaps three months, the boards could sit monthly except in cases of emergency.

(2) The practice of employers paying period money, in place of piecework payments, for awkward jobs arising during certain cargo discharging operations should ceases it tends to undermine the piecework system. Period money should only be paid for those jobs that warrant it—e.g. dirty and obnoxious cargoes like wet skins. All other jobs should be paid on an increased tonnage basis.

(3) A new piecework rate system should be introduced into the port transport industry. Instead of the registered port employers paying in the men's wages, plus 15% to 18% to the National Dock Labour Board, the deduction should be passed to the port labour

authority. Each commodity should have two piece-work rates:

(i) The contractor's rate, and;
(ii) The port labour authority's rate. The present method of paying each man a percentage of the gang's total day or shift earnings on the basis of so much per ton dead weight is satisfactory in principle. But what has happened in practice is that over the years the whole piecework structure has been thrown out of balance by an unequal distribution of the percentage increases on the basic piecework rates.

The result is that today there is no proper relationship between *work* and effort and the financial reward: the harder one works in fact, the less one receives for one's effort, with the result that the easier jobs now bring the highest financial return (compare, for example, some of the rates in the price book for the loading of bag work). Under the completely revised wage structure proposed, registered labour would receive a guaranteed weekly wage. This wage could then be broken down, as under the present system, into a day work rate for day workers and a piece rate plus time allowances for piece workers. Piece workers would continue to be paid either dead weight or measurement tonnage rates through the port labour authority. The port labour authority would itself operate a second rate for each commodity—the effort in this way for men working on low priced piece work operations (e.g. bag work) would be subsidised by the men employed on the better priced operations (e.g. the loading cars). Such a system would help to stabilise and level out the wages of port workers, and it would stop men from receiving high wages for doing very little, and others from earning low wages for considerably more effort, either physical or mental.

(4) A new system of loading rates is required, and quay gangs should be paid a percentage of the ship gangs' earnings. If this were done the quay gangs would be encouraged to cooperate more closely with the ship gangs to their mutual advantage. At present the quay gangs are paid dead weight tonnage, and the ship gangs are paid according to the commodity being worked: it is only natural that the quay gang will concentrate on the cargo that will benefit them most, i.e. the heavy cargo. One has to be a down holder to realise what this can mean.

(5) Administrative costs would be greatly reduced if the present National Dock Labour Board wage system were incorporated into a Port Labour Authority, with all employees' wages being administered by the new Port Authority as suggested on page four above.

(ix) Shift Work

Shift work on a three-shift system should be considered both by the employers and the men:

(1) The shift hours of work could be:

    (a) 6:30 a.m. to 2:30 p.m. with half hour meal break;

    (b) 2:30 p.m. to 10:30 p.m. with half hour meal break;

    (c) 10:30 p.m. to 6:30 a.m.

(2) Overtime should only be worked by the 2:30 p.m.– 10:30 p.m. shift if it will enable them to complete a ship due to sail on the morning tide, and provided that such overtime does not last beyond midnight.

(3) There should be only one shift worked on Saturdays and Sundays, to be taken by the various gangs based on a rota. This would ensure that every man had at least one full day off each week, and that seven-day working could be continued.

(4) Men working the full ten hours of the day shift throughout the week should not be permitted to work at weekends. Day workers could be used in any capacity during the week; e.g.:

  (a) As delivery or striking gangs;

  (b) As auxiliary ships gangs—i.e. as double banking gangs or as gangs for discharging light holds—holds that warrant day gangs only;

  (c) As ship-side gangs supplementary to the ship-gangs working over-side on the other two shifts;

  (d) As travelling gangs for striking and delivery work.

(5) The shift changeovers should be :

  (a) Day work gangs finishing on Friday evening at 5:00 p.m. or 7:00 p.m. would start their next shift at 6:30 a.m. on the following Monday.

  (b) The 6:30 a.m. shift would finish at 2:30 p.m. on Friday unless asked to work from 6:30 a.m. to 2:30 p.m. on Saturday.

  (c) The shift finishing at 10:30 p.m. on Friday would be eligible for Sunday overtime from 8:00 a.m. to 4:30 p.m.

(6) This kind of shift work system would give greater flexibility of labour with the minimum of inconvenience to both the employers and the employees in the port transport industry. From the point of view of the men the only inconvenient shift

would be that from 2:30 p.m.–10:30 p.m, but since it would be only necessary for them to work this shift once every three weeks there seems to be no reason why, if properly approached, they should not accept such a system. Shift work should first be introduced on a voluntary basis and on a limited scale, and the men should be asked to cooperate in ironing out any difficulties and in reducing any possible conflicts.

(x) Supervision

Under the new Port Labour Authorities, two grades of supervision should be introduced:

(1) The "transit shed" or "warehouse foreman" should continue to be recruited from office staff; the duties of the warehouse foreman would be to take responsibility (as at present) for all the goods directed to his "transit shed" or "warehouse", and to be responsible for the documentation as it relates to the "housed cargo".

(2) The "mobile labour foreman" should be recruited from amongst the registered port workers; having been selected for a specific job, his duties would entail drawing up a shed or warehouse stowage plan for the cargo due and then, bearing in mind his delivery plan, indenting the Labour Office of the Port Labour Authority for the men he will need to carry out the work; he must then inform the gangers allocated to him of his proposed method of work.

With the Port Labour Authority responsible for the deployment of labour, there would be a considerable reduction in administrative costs as labour could now be directed as and when required at any particular time. This would also rule out the need for contractor quay foremen as the Port Labour Authority's mobile labour foremen would be responsible for the landing and delivery; and striking and loading of all cargoes received into the sheds or warehouses, to which he may be seconded. This would not mean that the present "contractor quay foremen" could be mobile labour foreman, but that they should work in close cooperation with the port authority's shed or warehouse foreman. If shift working were to be introduced it would be necessary to recruit and train more foremen. It is essential that all labour foremen shall be recruited off the port labour register, this would give the men on the labour pool a chance of promotion to posts of junior management status, as well as drawing on the practical work experience of these men; such experience could then be strengthened by internal training programmes.

(xi) Suggestion Schemes

Suggestion schemes should be introduced to the port transport industry, to utilise any ideas that will speed up the work in the docks, or that will produce safer working conditions. In order to operate such a scheme successfully:

(1) A committee composed of employers and workers representatives should be set up;

(2) This committee should make awards for any suggestions that are accepted;

(3) The committee should state in writing their reasons for accepting or rejecting any particular suggestion.

(xii) The Trade Union Function

Nobody in their right mind would suggest that the trade unions in the port transport industry are in control of their membership. If they are to regain the leadership and respect of the port registered workers, the trade unions must reacquaint itself with the 'real' problems facing dock workers, and must resolve the chaos resulting *from* the present lack of effective official leadership. In the eyes of many of the men the trade unions are too concerned with working through the Dock Labour Board as a kind of "labour master" to concern themselves with the working problems of their members.

There are several ways in which the trade union could regain its lost prestige **in** the docks:

(1) The trade unions should set up an individual branch for each dock;

(2) Every man employed in a particular sector should be transferred onto the register of that sector's branch; in this way minority groups would be swallowed up in the new branches and would thus be prevented from being able to control the majority as often happens at present.

(3) The system, used by the employers in the engineering industry, of allowing selection and election annually of stewards to represent the work people should be introduced into all British ports; such persons should be elected on a dock basis, and should be called "dock stewards"; their authority would be limited to the dock sector that elected them, and their function would be to deal with small internal problems of general interest arising in their dock sector. On no account should any unofficial Port or National Dock Stewards Committee he allowed to establish itself outside the control of the parent trade unions. Any dock stewards who

attempted to form such a committee without the blessing of their trade union should be considered to have forfeited their position as dock stewards.

(4) As an alternative to the scheme outlined above for electing dock stewards, Dock Committees could be formed. The representatives on these committees would be elected by the registered port workers within a given sector; the sectors could be formed on a quota basis—e.g. each dock force of 500 men, selected on the basis of their work numbers, would be entitled to elect one representative to the dock committee. Numbers 34000 to 34499; numbers 34500 to 35000 etc. would each elect one committee member. In this way each group in the docks would have a channel for complaints and grievances and access to means of remedying their problems. The function of the dock committees would be to receive complaints and queries, and approaching the appropriate authority in order to find, where possible, an agreeable solution. Each dock committee should be provided with a meeting room and a competent person to act as secretary; the committees should elect their own chairmen.

1. In each port there should be set up a Port Committee, this committee would be formed from members elected in each of the docks within the port, four members from each dock, two representing the employees and two representing the employers. The objects of such committees would be:

(a) For the port workers representatives to put forward any complaints or problem that the dock worker committees are not able to resolve,